Keja did not like the burning heat that attacked the top of his head. He glanced up and saw the archway again. He frowned and carefully stowed the key between his belt and tunic. The Gate disappeared. Keja touched the key lightly.

The archway reappeared. It wavered, clearer now. Keja whirled about in joy.

"The Gate of Paradise! I've found it!" Visions of lovely houris raced through his mind, courtesans serving him iced wines and popping succulent tidbits into his waiting mouth, noble ladies with an intense yearning for all he had to offer. "The Gate! It wasn't a fool's chase. It was real!" He stood back and stared at the arch. Large runes across the top boldly proclaimed: THE GATE OF PARADISE. Puzzling out the smaller inscription required too much effort. Keja vowed to study it at length. Later. For now the Gate of Paradise was his and his alone!

THE FLAME KEY

KEYS TO PARADISE
BOOK I

DANIEL MORAN

THE FLAME KEY

A TOM DOHERTY ASSOCIATES BOOK

THE FLAME KEY

Copyright © 1987 by Daniel Moran

First printing: April 1987

A TOR BOOK

Published by Tom Doherty Associates, Inc.
49 West 24 Street
New York, N.Y. 10010

Cover art by Judith Mitchell
Cover design by Carol Russo

ISBN: 0-812-54600-8
CAN. ED.: 0-812-54601-6

PRINTED IN THE UNITED STATES OF AMERICA

0 9 8 7 6 5 4 3 2 1

To Anna

Chapter One

Giles Grimsmate hungrily tore a piece of coarse black bread from the round loaf in front of him. He used it to sop up the last of the salty fish stew from his wooden bowl. It had been a long while since he had found food this good—or surroundings so pleasant.

A young serving maid grinned at him as she removed his bowl and spoon. "Lick the bowl?" the shapely brunette asked, her words falling like honey.

He had been away from people far too long, Giles decided, when even a simple comment aroused him. He took a swipe at her behind as she turned away, but she dodged with practiced skill and did a saucy dance step on her way back to the kitchen. The weather-battered man wiped his mouth on a many-times-patched sleeve that had seen better days—and worse, too.

He marveled again at how long it had been since he had eaten such a good meal. And fish was far from his favorite food. There had been little else during the War, but it had filled his belly well enough while others starved. Giles took a slender white bone from the pouch at his side. He turned from the table and rested his back against the wall, putting his legs up along the bench. Contentedly, he surveyed the room as he picked his teeth.

The room in The Laughing Cod was warm and comfortable and gave a respite from sleeping under hedges, which would only drip cold rain on him all night. Giles decided the presence of others gave a touch of the

tonic he needed. He'd been alone with only his thoughts
for comfort more than he cared to remember these past
twenty years.

The maid returned, running a wet rag across the table
to clean up spilled stew and bread crumbs that had
escaped his voracious appetite.

"A flagon of ale when you have a moment, please,"
he said.

"La-de-dah, isn't he the polite one?"

Giles saw that the small courtesy pleased her, however.
She stopped her table-cleaning chores and scurried off to
draw the ale, returning almost immediately.

"The ale goes on the bill," he said, "but this is for
you." He laid a coin on the table. She scooped it up; it
disappeared into an apron pocket. Her smile warmed
Giles more than the strong ale puddling in his stomach.
He sighed. He was getting old—had gotten old. And
what did he have to show for it save scars, gray-shot
black hair and memories?

Memories. Good. Bad. And even worse than bad.

Giles took a hefty drink from the pewter flagon as he
studied the maid. His wife had had a smile like that when
he first met her. Full red lips, white teeth and a smile
that melted his soul. Giles drank heavily and remembered
better days. Days when his two sons were born, days
when Leorra was young and passionately supple in his
arms, when he owned a plot of good, rich farmland and a
horse and a cow, and rights to grazing outside the
village.

That was all before the Trans War. For twenty long,
bitter years he had fought in that accursed war. And what
had it accomplished? A dead family. The wife he loved
killed in a raid on his village. His boys dead because the
War lasted overlong, and they had grown to fighting size.
Giles closed pale gray eyes and felt his pulse thundering
like war drums in his head. They had been sent off to the
brutal eastern provinces, where the fighting had been

fiercest, and they had never returned. Word came eventually that they were buried somewhere near Gallania and that they had died honorably. After twenty years of senseless death, he remained unconvinced that any of it—the war, the raids, the battles, the killing—was honorable.

Only the leaders had profited greatly from the Trans War. Playing on emotions and creating prejudices where none had existed before, they had prolonged the War. Cleverly, they had manipulated people, acquired territory, and avenged themselves on old enemies. But above all else, they had become richer and richer. What did they care that men and women had died, both Trans and humans?

The War had ground to a halt, both sides depleted of troops and heartsick from the killing and endless suffering. Mass desertion, the leaders had called it. Sanity was the only word appropriate. Still, the commanders had not protested. Their games of conquest and wealth-seeking only turned down different avenues.

Giles sincerely hoped that others found some peace when they returned home. He certainly hadn't. He had found his plot and his house—devoid of everything that he had loved. He took another deep draft of the ale. It did nothing to erase the pain of that homecoming.

The village elders were no longer elder. They were young upstarts with ideas contrary to his own. Oh, yes, they made room for the grizzled veteran on the governing council. They gave a small celebration in honor of his return and grudgingly moved in an extra seat for the council meetings. The meetings were filled with endless bickering over the most trivial of matters, accomplishing little more than making Giles angry. He soon quit attending.

He didn't know the villagers anymore. He couldn't make friends with them because few were his age, and fewer still had shared the constant hardships and had experienced the ineffable bonds of friendship forged by trooping.

Giles put away his toothpick and took out a plain, well-used darkwood pipe. He filled it carefully with tobacco shaved from a block. Clouds of noxious blue smoke enveloped him, and he stared into it, oblivious of the activity and conversations in the room.

Six months had proved to him that he could no longer call the village home. He had rolled up his blankets, made a small pack of his few belongings, got his boots repaired and left quietly. He imagined that the village sighed in relief when they found him gone.

Giles puffed deeply, the smoke filling tired lungs and bringing back a tantalizing hint of youth. For just a moment, to be sure, but he felt it. These past months had been nothing but aimless wandering, little better than staying in his village.

He walked, he rode, he traveled, and yet memories of Leorra still haunted him. And his sons. And the good life now evaporated because of the War, because he had believed and fought and found only misery.

What had he accomplished? Early this afternoon he had come down into this delta town along the coast. Klepht, they called it. It seemed no better or worse than a dozen other seaports.

As he had ambled along the waterfront, Giles had been amused by the inn sign. THE LAUGHING COD, it proclaimed. The artist had portrayed a plump fish with its fins on its waist and a mouth open in what had to be a loud guffaw. Giles had entered only to have an ale, but it was such excellent ale that he had found himself taking a room for the night. He had a few coins jingling in his pouch and no schedule to keep. Why not enjoy a night at the inn, someone else's cooking, sleeping in a real bed, and maybe a moment's conversation? It had been too long since he had a decent traveling companion to argue with, to swap lies with, to depend on.

Giles puffed harder as the tobacco burned down to spent embers. Outside, the sun set and cast cool gray fingers of twilight through the cobblestoned streets of Klepht. The inn slowly filled with sailors and fishermen whose day of hard labor had ended.

Giles sat listening to the talk of nets and gear and the catch and cargo. He shared little with these men, but the dim reflections of their companionship proved better than being alone for another night.

In a quiet moment, he signaled for another flagon. When the maid brought it, he asked, "Do they ever talk of anything but the sea?"

She ran her hand through the thick mat of her curly brown hair. "No. But they'll slow down pretty quick and begin to dice. Do you have any skill?"

"Not much, but a spot of luck rides at my shoulder now and again," Giles said. "What's the game?"

"Anadromi. Do you know it?"

"Never heard of it." Giles flexed arthritic fingers until they snapped as loud as any cannon shot. They felt up to a game of dice, as they had on many a night with his men during the War.

"I'm sure they'll teach you. Go easy or they'll have all your money. You won't be able to pay your bill, and I'll have to put up with you as scullery maid for the next week."

"Is that so bad?"

"You'd look a perfect fright wearing a dress and apron," the brunette said, white teeth gleaming.

"You've convinced me to be careful. My knees are not nearly as comely as yours." He settled back and sipped his ale. Warm, dry, full, content, a bit of harmless flirting. Not much more a man could ask for when his world had become a hollow shell.

The talk washing around Giles slowed, and the men of the sea quieted, contemplating their burning bowls and their memories.

At last, a stubby little man at a table raised his fist and waggled it back and forth. The serving maid nodded and took a leather cup from the shelf behind the serving counter. She brought it to the table and shook it several times before rolling six bone-white dice out on the table. She bent over to see what she had rolled.

"Not bad," she said. "Maybe I should play tonight?"

The stubby man grinned up at her. "And who'd serve the ale?" he asked.

"Why, you would, of course."

"Get yer out of here now," the man said.

Giles assumed this was an oft-repeated dialogue that had become a ritual, and once again he longed for the steady companionship of good friends.

The man dumped the dice back into the leather cup and rattled it twice. He rolled the dice out, looked at them and shook his head glumly. For a time, he seemed to be the only one in the room interested. He rolled them again and again, shaking his head and muttering every time he examined the results.

"You can't fool us, Niss. When you shake your head like that, everyone knows you're netting the big fish." Chuckles rolled around the room.

"Just tryin' to warm them up a bit. Come along and help, Tal."

Several men went to the table. Each took his turn at rolling the dice, warming the leather cup with their hands before each toss.

Giles left the warmth of his spot to wander over, standing back and watching the results of the rolls.

"Are you ready, lads? It's time to be serious." The little man looked around the circle of men at the table. Then he glanced up at Giles. "They hang back. What of you, stranger?"

"I don't know the game," Giles said. "Let me watch for a bit till I see what it's about."

The man shrugged, going back to rattling the dice in

what he hoped was an enticing fashion. He passed the cup to his left. The men rolled once around the table to see who would begin.

For a half hour Giles watched. It was not a game he had seen before but wasn't difficult to understand. It had to do with runs of numbers in ascending order and differed little from a game played in camps during his days of soldiering.

Two players lost consistently and bowed out of the game. Five men still sat at the table. Niss gestured to Giles and to an empty seat. Giles nodded and sat down.

For a time Giles' losses equaled his winnings. As the game became more familiar, he decided there was little strategy to learn for Anadromi, unlike some he had played that involved multiple rolls and decisions of which die to leave and which to roll again.

A big, burly man had a good run of luck and reduced the players' ranks to only four. The pile of small coins slowly grew in front of Giles, but the gnarled seaman won consistently. On the next round Niss dropped out, sweeping his few remaining coins back into his pouch. "The luck's not with me tonight," he said. "Mousie seems to have the most of it."

Giles grinned at him. "Maybe another night."

"Aye, there's always another night."

On the next round, a young, round-faced, red-bearded man followed Niss' example.

Giles looked at the burly seaman. "You ready to call it quits?" he asked.

"Not on your life," Mousie growled. "I'm looking to hook the big fish tonight. I'll take your money as well as the next man's." He glowered at Giles.

Giles shrugged, picked up his coins and let them slip neatly from his thick fingers into a stack on the table. "Your choice," he said. "Let'em roll."

Mousie shoved half of his coins into the center of the table. Giles matched them. But luck was beginning to abandon the seaman. The dice rolled out and stopped. A triple six, a three, and a one. That was an excellent roll for many different games, but not this one. Giles' roll fared scarcely better, but it won the round.

The seaman shoved the rest of his stack out, and Giles matched it again. As winner of the previous round, he rolled first—a nearly perfect roll. Two, three, three, four, five, six.

Giles felt no sense of triumph, only a quiet pleasure at the roll. He had outgrown youthful enthusiasm over such matters. "You give up? It looks like a tough one to beat." He passed the cup to Mousie.

Two fists enclosed the cup and shook it vigorously. The fisherman concentrated on the rattling dice, willing them to obey his mumbled commands. Giles relaxed, knowing full well that there was nothing he could do about six cubes of bone with black spots on them.

The men in the inn sensed the drama at the table and gathered to watch the roll. When the dice came spinning out of the cup and slid to a stop, a sigh passed through the crowd. Giles had won again.

Mousie stared around him as if he couldn't comprehend what had happened, then looked at the pile of coins in front of Giles. For a moment, he seemed about to fling himself over it.

"Let me see those bones."

Giles silently passed him the leather cup. The man stared moodily into it, then upended it, spilling the dice out onto the table. One by one he picked them up, examining them as if he suspected that Giles had substituted them for the real dice. Finally he looked up at Giles. "I want a chance to get me money back."

"I gave you a chance to quit. Didn't you keep anything back?"

"No," the man muttered.

"That's foolish. Then you've got nothing left to wager, have you?"

The sailor said nothing, staring off toward the fireplace. Making a hard decision, he tugged open the neck of his sailor's smock and pulled a string from around his neck. A key dangled from the string.

Mousie pulled the string over his head and handed it to Giles. "I'll wager this against the whole pile," he said.

Giles turned the key over in his hands. It appeared to be gold. The three teeth were square and the circular shank stretched nearly four inches, ending with a flat round circle. In the center of the circle rode a small, light green gemstone; peridot, Giles thought. Encircling the stone were finely etched runes.

"You're sure you want to wager this?" Giles asked.

Mousie nodded glumly.

"It looks valuable. Gold, isn't it?"

"Yes."

"Where'd you get it?"

"A friend. He left it to me. We were shipmates once. He was killed in the War. He'd understand me wagering it." Mousie snorted derisively. "Old Porgg bet more'n this in his day. Best two out of three rolls?"

Giles turned the key over in his hands, thinking. He had won all the sailor's money, plus some from each of the other players. Now this man wanted a chance to win it back. Luck was with Giles tonight, and for the most part, it was other men's money.

He nodded. "Two out of three. Your key against my coins." Giles felt more alive than he had in weeks. "Want to roll one die to see who goes first?"

Mousie won the roll of the single die and grinned, as if he had already won. He dumped the six dice into the cup and shook it with confidence.

But it ended quickly. Giles won both rounds and pocketed the key.

The sailor stood up, knocking over the bench. "You cheated me," he yelled.

The room grew quiet. Mousie's work-roughened hands

clenched at his sides. Giles stood quietly, pushing his pouch around to the back of his belt so that it wouldn't be in his way. As casual as the gesture was, it carried professionalism and deadly resignation with it. Giles' mind settled into fighting calm as he appraised his would-be foe.

He realized that the rest of the men in the room had backed off, watching silently.

"Easy now, friend," Giles said. "I gave you the chance to quit twice. I asked if you were sure you wanted to bet."

The man's face flamed. "You cheated!" he roared.

"You can't cheat in this game," Giles said. "It's all luck. You checked the dice."

A call came from the corner of the room. "That's right, Mousie. You know you can't cheat in that game. The stranger won, right squarely."

"But it's not fair," Mousie argued. "He took all my money."

"I didn't take it. You wagered it and lost," Giles said.

The man shook his head, not wanting to believe what he had done.

"Come on, friend. Sit down and share a brandy, and we'll talk about it." Giles raised his voice. "Landlord, brandy here for me and my friend. Brandy for everyone!"

A cheer went up around the room. The landlord looked at Giles as if to reassure himself that the stranger meant it. Giles nodded. The expression on his face made the innkeeper blanch. He had seen veterans before, that look, the deadly quality they carried with them wherever they went.

Mousie looked around him at the beaming faces. He didn't want to believe that his mates were abandoning him. Giles reached across the table and laid his hand on the other man's thick arm.

"Come. Sit down and have a brandy. We'll work something out. I don't want to take your last coin. I've been without a hope, much less a pair of coppers to rub together. I know what it's like."

The man stared up at Giles to see if he was serious. The serving maid quietly set glasses of brandy on the table and scurried away. Mousie watched her go, a perplexed look on his dull face. Finally, with a sigh, he righted the bench and sat down. He picked up the glass of brandy and swallowed it with one gulp. Giles shoved the second glass over to him.

"Go ahead. She'll bring more. Drink it down, then we'll talk."

The second brandy took two gulps. The crimson wrath had gone out of Mousie's face. Giles was certain that he no longer wanted to fight. He fingered the coins and key on the table.

"You shouldn't have continued to gamble until you lost everything. Excuse me for saying so, but that's a stupid thing to do."

Chagrined, Mousie hung his head.

"I don't want you to go hungry before the next catch," Giles said. "I'm not giving it all back. After all, I did win fairly." He let the coins riffle from his cupped, callused fingers. "Maybe next time you'll be more cautious. But probably not, eh?"

Mousie stared at Giles, then laughed. "Probably not. This is not the first time."

"I suspected so." Giles shoved a stack of five coins over to Mousie. "See if you can hang on to that for a week. Friends?"

Mousie stared bemusedly at the coins in front of him. He reached out and grasped Giles' hand. "Friends," he said.

Giles slipped the key and the rest of the coins into his pouch and stood. "I'll be back and drink with you later. I need to speak to the landlord."

When he had finished assuring the landlord that he would stand brandy for all, Giles retired to his place by the fireplace. Stranger things had happened to him. While he had not been afraid of the sailor, Giles was pleased that he had been able to placate him. He wasn't sure that he could have bested the burly sailor, even knowing a thousand ways of fighting learned over a lifetime. Bumps and bruises were a thing of his past. He could do well without them.

Giles reached into his pouch and pulled out the key. Leaning forward to catch the light from the fire, he examined it more closely. It *was* gold, and the small peridot caught the dancing firelight and winked at him, as if sharing a wondrous secret.

The runic inscription ran in a tight circle around the small stone. Giles puzzled it out, rune by rune. THE KEY TO PARADISE, it read. Giles frowned.

A man much older than Giles limped over to the table. He carried his tumbler of brandy with him.

"I came to thank you for the brandy, stranger. It warms these poor old bones. May I sit with you?"

Giles gestured to the empty bench opposite. He looked at the key again and started to place it back in his pouch.

The old man's wizened, blue-veined hand reached across the table. "May I?" he asked.

Giles laid the key in the man's outstretched palm.

After careful scrutiny, he returned the key to Giles. "I thought so. The key to Paradise."

"So I read," Giles said. "What does it mean?"

"Don't you know?" The old man looked to see if Giles poked fun at him.

"It means nothing to me."

"I could tell you a story, but my throat's dry," he said slyly, feigning a harsh cough. Giles raised his hand to summon the serving maid. He pointed to the old man's glass.

"Ah, you're a rare one, sir. Thankee. Now, as to the key to Paradise. Somewhere out there is the Gate of Paradise, and if we can believe the tales, this key will unlock that gate. Now, what's behind the Gate . . . ah, the stories! Gold, jewels, beautiful women, power, wealth . . . your heart's desire! Nobody knows, but the stories say that it's everything you could ever want.''

"Do they? And just where is this Gate of Paradise?''

"Ah, there's the rub. Every story I've heard puts it in a different place. North, south, east and west. Take your choice. Might be it's in all those places—or none.''

"Sounds like just another tall tale to me,'' Giles said. "Have you ever heard of anyone who actually saw the Gate?''

"No,'' the old man admitted. "But this fits the story, too. The story runs that you've got to have the key in your hand to actually see the Gate.''

Giles threw back his head and laughed.

"You laugh, sir. But people believe this story. I do. And here you are with the key in your hand. Best keep it safe—unless your charity extends to offering an old crippled man the key as a token.''

"I spent twenty years at the Wars. Promoted to sergeant and broken to the ranks three times. Through it all, I learned one lesson: be generous to beggars, but not *too* generous.'' The grizzled veteran stood, saying, "Your story is worth another brandy. But no more. I'm off for a drink with my erstwhile gambling partner, and then to bed. Thank you for your company. Come round tomorrow night and I'll buy you another.'' He laid his hand on the old man's shoulder.

After a quick drink with Mousie, Giles paid the landlord, and mounted the stairs to his room above.

The wind had blown the threatening storm clouds away, and Giles stood at his window for a brief while, looking down over the moonlight-silvered waterfront.

The night had been unexpectedly profitable, and had provided a moment's diversion in what had become a life of pointless drifting. Pointless. No home, nothing to tie him down. Giles rubbed his aching joints, wishing the storm would come and get it over. The promise of rain only protracted his pains. He stretched, yawned, and thought of the fable the old man had told. Absurd maunderings, nothing more than superstition. Giles had heard it all before, in dozens of places, over the years.

And what if it were true? Riches to carry him into his old age, which wasn't so far off. He straightened his right arm, wincing as joints protested even this small movement.

Giles kicked off his boots and lay down on the bed, pulling the covers over himself. The Gate of Paradise. Why not go looking for it? He had nowhere else to go or anything of a pressing nature. Why not wander with a purpose? But no hurry, no hurry.

Those were his last thoughts before his eyes closed for the night. By the time the rains pelted wet and cold against the window, Giles Grimsmate snored loudly, his dreams about Paradise.

Chapter Two

The Leather Cup was deceptively quiet even though it stood just a block off Klepht's main street. A few laborers from the shipyards stopped in to end their working day, but they lingered only long enough to drink a couple mugs of watery ale. One by one, they shouldered their tool bags and departed, worn men on their way home to families. Some would be met with love, others with the shrilling of wives and the sniveling of children. None noticed the small, dark, quick-gestured man lounging in one cobwebbed corner of the tavern.

An oddly cheerless lot, Keja Tchurak thought, even for such an undistinguished delta town. Not for the first time, Keja volubly cursed the treacherously unkind fate that had driven him from a comfortable berth and a willing woman and sent him fleeing, to hide from shadows, to jump at the slightest of sounds behind him. But such kept him free—and alive.

He cut a bite-sized morsel of beef from the greasy slab on the plate before him. It was awful, nearly tasteless.

Keja leaned back, chewing thoughtfully. Rosaal had been quite a woman. Raven hair, long slender legs so willing to part for him, the sumptuous body of a courtesan. He stopped chewing as he remembered with fondness their nights together. It had been a favor of the gods that her family had ample money, too. That she showed herself to be a bit on the dimwitted side rankled after a few passionate nights, though. Eventually Keja had become sated enough to realize that her body and loving ways weren't everything.

Keja resumed chewing. The tough beef required many swallows of ale to get it down. The bread was a little better, but even it wasn't fresh. Yesterday's, probably. Keja hated inns where the owner took so little pride in what he served. No doubt this accounted for the other patrons simply swilling the pitiful ale and then leaving to go tup their mistresses or wives. That's what Keja would be doing, had he mistress or wife, rather than sitting in The Leather Cup.

He looked around the nearly empty room. Not good. If the city guard came a'checking, he would stand out like red silk bows on a swine's snout. He prayed for a quick change in the innkeeper's penurious policies, for good ale and food, for the room to fill up. Perhaps some locals would come in after their suppers and a lusty roll with their mistresses. That would make it easier to remain inconspicuous. If patrons didn't show up soon, Keja saw no choice but to retire to his dismal room upstairs.

He tried another bite of beef. As he feared, it had not improved. Keja waved to the serving wench to take it away. "Bring me a couple of hard-boiled eggs," he ordered imperiously. "This beef is a disgrace even to the bottom of Klepht's sewer, if there is one." He pointed to his cup. "And another ale."

The serving wench said nothing, accepting his order with ill-concealed bitterness. Keja watched her walk away with a gracefulness no human shared. A Trans, and part cat. He hadn't seen many in Klepht. Keja eyed her critically and decided she'd be a pretty one if the landlord didn't keep her on the run so much. She was a bit disheveled, her hair mussed and a streak of soot ran across her forehead, probably from stoking the kitchen fire. But she was slender, with clean, sharp features, and that unmistakable feline quality in walk and gesture. Keja shivered a little when he saw her yellow eyes with vertical slit pupils; definitely catlike—and predatory.

Keja wondered what it would be like with her, all night long, releasing those animal passions. He had heard tales of lovemaking with a Trans. Keja had to admit the idea excited him.

The cat Trans serving maid returned with his ale and two speckled brown eggs rocking to and fro in a small wooden bowl. He picked one and rapped it against the side of the bowl. Egg white oozed out onto his fingers. He glanced up at her. Those fierce yellow cat eyes shone with defiance, daring him to complain again.

Keja shoved the bowl away, then silently picked up his ale and carried it over to the fireplace, standing with his back to the flames. The young man felt nothing but disgust at the service, at Klepht, at everything. Under different circumstances, he would have complained loud and long. Not now. He dared not. He peered across the room, trying to study the weather outside, but the windows were too dirty.

Keja needed to get away from this provincial jerkwater town, to keep on the move. At the moment, however, he needed rest. He had been hounded too long. This slovenly inn provided him a good enough respite; it was not the sort of place guards would expect an accomplished thief like the great Keja Tchurak to choose for accommodations.

Keja's left arm still ached where one of Werlink l'Karm's personal guards had sliced it with a lucky thrust. Idly, he rubbed it. It hadn't hurt this badly in days. It must be turning to rain outside.

Keja smiled. Master thief that he was, he'd escaped, and with a tidy haul, too. But l'Karm didn't give up easily. The merchant's private guard had dogged Tchurak's steps at every turn, and only overwhelming cleverness had saved him on several occasions. But Keja had to admit that when they closed in on him along the River

Kale, escape had come through pure luck. The story he had told the old fisherman about jilting a lover rang true, but the fisherman being at the right place could only be called luck. Hiding under a wagonload of fish was not at all pleasant but seemed like high times at Gresham's Fair in comparison with what the guards would have done to him.

And the haul had stayed intact. A hefty bag of coin, some baubles he would sell off when he got to a bigger city, and the gold key. If he had thrown the guard off his trail, and it looked as if he had, he might follow up the chimerical story behind the key told to him by loving, lovely Rosaal.

His backside good and warm from the fire, Keja sighed at the memory of the fiery Rosaal gracing his bed, then wandered back to a bench near the corner. Locals drifted in, bringing with them gusts of fresh air from the windy weather without.

Keja ordered another ale and watched the locals playing a board game. They were a quiet lot, glum and dour. They played with too much seriousness for his tastes.

He reached into his pouch and pulled forth the golden key. His thoughts drifted far from booty or key. Unconsciously, Keja turned the key over and over in his hand.

"You need to bring in more wood from outside, and there's two hands up out there looking for their ale." The landlord's loud, grating voice stirred instant dislike in Keja. He had heard that tone too many times, times when he had been down on his luck and actually had done menial tasks to survive. "When you've done that, the baking pans haven't been washed from yesterday. And don't give me any of your dark looks, my Pet."

"Don't call me Pet."

Keja looked from the Trans serving wench to the landlord. The way the light caught her face highlighted the cat-portion over the human. He wondered if she would rip out the insulting landlord's throat. If Keja had been in her place, he would have.

The landlord of The Leather Cup wiped greasy hands across the expanse of his apron and laughed. "Don't we have our pride? Get on with you. Don't stand idle." He turned back to stir a pot of ill-smelling stew.

Petia Darya made an obscene gesture behind his back and stormed into the taproom to fill two cups for the thirsty patrons. She'd been working at the inn for a week and would stay only long enough to earn a few coins before moving on. Servitude did not suit her at all.

She carried the brimming cups across the room to the men who scowled at her. They were the same two who had harassed her all week.

"Filthy Trans bitch," one muttered as she turned away.

Petia had the desire to turn and show them a bit of her cat nature, but she subdued her temper. Petia vowed to get her revenge, not only on them, but the landlord too. Soon.

Two more men came in and ordered, and for the next few minutes she busily fetched ale. By the time she caught up with the orders, her anger only smoldered.

She brought wood in from outside until her arms ached, then set to washing the baking pans. She was interrupted from time to time with calls for more ale. The landlord was being his usual obsequious self to the customers, but drawing and serving was beneath his dignity—which he let her know at every turn. Petia was kept busy between kitchen and the public room.

She wished that she were anywhere except here in Klepht. Petia had left Trois Havres in a hurry, her burglaries too careless. It was a case of overconfidence. If she had not seen the handbill seeking her arrest, she might now be working off seven years in the duke's gold mines. Luck had come her way when she found a ship crossing the Everston Sea and a cargomaster willing to look the other way for a few coins to augment his paltry wages.

Escape had not been without other penalties. She had arrived in Bericlere with only a few coins to show for all the troubles besetting her. Petia stoically accepted that; it was part of her heritage. Trois Havres, her home and home of many of the Trans, was pleasant enough but had few opportunities for the ambitious. Petia almost sneered at the idea of ambition in a Trans.

For over two hundred years they had been scorned, reviled, made into little more than slaves by a sorceress far too quick with her curses. Lady Cassia n'Kaan had turned the people of an entire continent into part human, part animal for a relatively minor offense. Petia often wondered if the broken trade treaty with Lord Lophar had, indeed, been the cause for so much misery for her and untold others turned into Trans. She guessed at more between sorceress and merchant-lord. It mattered little now. The sorceress had perished, and the Trans had slowly evolved, regressing to human form.

And she had been indentured and escaped, become a thief and escaped, and now Petia tried her hand at serving. From this she'd escape, too.

Petia held out a hand and sharp talons snapped out like the blade of an opening folding knife. The Trans became more human with every passing generation, but many traits remained. For that, Petia thanked gods living, dead, and to be.

Because of the partial humanity, Petia and the others of her kind worked harder to prove themselves, to get ahead, to survive. That driving ambition had provided fuel for the Trans War. A demagogue with honeyed voice and inflammatory mind arose to condemn the Trans for economic setbacks. Even now, even after twenty years and more, Petia felt anger rising at Duke Pattch. His coin was not of gold but of hatred.

For all those dying during twenty years of fighting,

Pattch lived, as did the other lords who had seized the opportunity for aggression. It became expedient to correct disputed boundaries, attack old enemies, and if one were strong enough, to acquire new territory.

Twenty years of war had worsened the commoners' lot and bettered those in power. And throughout it all, the Trans still bore the brunt of it. Hatred, illogical or not, festered and corrupted even the most decent of men. Few on either side escaped.

Petia Darya did not escape, nor did she want to. Especially with humans such as this foolish, fat landlord to fan the fires of her prejudices.

She finished the last baking pan and set it on the wooden rack to dry. As much as it rankled, Petia knew she must clean up after the patrons. They were little better than pigs—and she knew many pig Trans who were impeccably clean compared to The Leather Cup's landlord and clientele.

Petia poured cold water into a bucket and then added hot water from the stove. A brick of hard soap would help to cut the grease. She couldn't believe those tables. Had anyone *ever* cleaned them before her? Were all humans so compulsively dirty? Without realizing it, she licked the back of her hand and drew it quickly across her face.

Petia started in the corner nearest the door. Several patrons had left, and those remaining clustered near the fire. She didn't blame them. It was drafty by the door, cold rain blowing in. The only thing she hated worse than being dirty was being wet.

Hot water, soap and hard work took off the grimy layer of rings from the beer mugs and grease from spilled stew. Petia worked slowly from table to table. Two more men left, leaving the door unlatched. It swung open in a gust of wind, and the landlord yelled at her to close it.

Petia obeyed, noticing the insolent man who had sent his beef back earlier in the evening. He silently moved

closer to the fireplace but did not settle in with the rest of
the group. From the corner of her eye, she saw he held
an object in his hands, turning it over and over.

She moved closer, still cleaning the table tops, until
curiosity got the better of her. She had to see the
glittering object. Probably some insignificant memento of
the war. A small knife, perhaps, or a coin. Something
that occasionally reflected a golden glint of firelight.

The Trans woman couldn't get a clear view, no matter
how she tried. Spying the empty ale mugs of the departed
customers, she quietly walked past his table and gathered
them up. Turning, she asked, "More ale for you this
evening, sir?"

He started, pulled from his reverie. "What? Oh, yes,
another."

Petia smiled happily. She had gotten a better look at
the object. It was a key—of solid gold, if she was any
judge.

As the ale gurgled from its barrel into the mug, Petia's
mind churned with plans. That man stayed at this inn.
His room above could be reached easily from the roof.
That room had a window that didn't stick, unlike some.
She had opened it only that morning to get fresh air while
doing the upstairs cleaning.

The gold key might unlock a new future for her. If
nothing else, it would get her away from the inn and the
doltish landlord.

She hurried back to the table where the man stared into
the ebbing fire. Petia set the frothing mug in front of
him, getting a closer look at the key. Gold. Definitely.
Thoughts of fencing it raced through her mind. She knew
one merchant in contraband over on the Street of Fins
who had a reputation for being almost honest. Twenty
percent of value? Could she barter for that much of the
key's true value? More?

Petia took up her rag and continued scrubbing tables.
For the first time in days she hummed tunelessly as she

worked. With luck and a modicum of caution, the key would be hers this night, and by morning she would be gone.

Sleep came easily to Petia. Fatigued from the long day's work, she curled up on a straw mat near the fire in the kitchen, pulling the thin wool blanket up to her chin. She concentrated for a moment, then closed her eyes, confident of awakening in a few hours.

It lacked a few minutes of the second watch of the night when Petia awoke. She stretched luxuriously, cat-like, loosening her limbs. Petia fashioned her hands into claws and smiled with satisfaction as her nails length-ened. There were some advantages to being a Trans, particularly a feline.

Petia tucked her bright red blouse inside her skirt, then hoisted the long, dark skirt above her knees. Taking hold of the front hem, she pulled it between her legs and tucked it into the back of her skirt waist. This gave freedom of movement and lessened the chances of getting caught on a protruding nail as she climbed.

Silently, she left the kitchen. For a moment, she stood near the tap, eyes adjusting to the darkened inn room, then she crossed the room to the outside door. She opened it noiselessly, slipped out and faded into the darkness.

Reaching up to the small gable over the door, she found the bracing and swung herself up. She crouched on the roof, thankful both wind and rain had quieted. She examined the roof for weak spots or betraying loose tiles.

The cold night air cleared her head. Petia felt alive, in her element. The night sky her sole companion, an empty roof, a guest with a rich prize at its end, the chance to use her light-fingered skills once again set her pulse racing. This was what life was meant to be, not running to every ale-guzzling, dirty human's beck.

Petia confidently traversed the sloping roof, angling up

to the main ridgepiece. Reaching it, she straddled it and caught her breath, listening for any sounds from the rooms beneath her feet.

Checking the downslope, she gauged the distance from the corner to the window of Keja's room. She hesitated, sinking into a dark shadow when she spotted the lantern of the night watch. The man checked the doors of businesses along his route and occasionally raised his lantern to peer down an alleyway. In less than a minute, he had passed on. Her sharp ears told of his steady progress away.

Moving more slowly now, Petia crept down the roof. Reaching the gutter, she lowered herself prone and peered over the edge. A smile darted across her thin lips. She had judged accurately. Less than a foot to her left opened the window of her prey.

She turned her body parallel with the roof edge and hooked her left knee and foot into the gutter. Reaching down, she grasped the windowframe with clawlike fingernails. After a small prayer to Dismatis, protector of thieves, she exerted pressure upward. The window slid open quietly. She gripped the gutter and swung herself down to the sill and into the room.

Petia moved sideways from the window like the hunting cat that she was. Never show a silhouette, should the man awaken. Unless the man had rearranged things, she knew the furniture's placement.

Where would he hide the key? His pouch? Most men kept their smaller valuables there. In the subtle light, Petia made out his clothes tossed over the back of a wooden chair. She moved silently to the chair, feeling cautiously for the clothing. He had removed his shirt last and it was on top. She picked it up and placed it over her arm. Beneath were his trousers, but she found no belt.

A smart one. She replaced the clothes and moved to the chest along one wall. It was a low, flat-topped cabinet only two drawers high.

Carefully, she felt along the top. The belt! But no pouch. She ran her fingers down the front of the cabinet, feeling for the drawer pulls. The top drawer slid open. Petia reached into it. Nothing. She closed it and reached for the handles of the second drawer.

A snore came from the bed, followed almost immediately by a coughing spell. Petia stood motionless, crouched over the lower drawer. The coughing stopped, and Petia continued her search. The sleeping man moaned once, then his breathing became regular again.

Petia's heartbeat slowed, and she pulled the bottom drawer open. Nothing.

Cautious soul, this one, she thought. The pouch must rest under his pillow. That called for a great deal more stealth. She looked toward the bed. He slept, oblivious to her presence.

Petia made her way to the foot of the bed and stood looking down at him. Outside, the scudding night clouds cleared to send silvery moonlight flooding through the room. During the evening, she had been much more interested in the object in his hands than in what he had looked like.

Not bad looking, she decided. For a human. But even in sleep, he had a demeanor that warned he should not be taken casually. Petia wondered if he might not be Trans, also. She felt an oddly compelling kinship with him; his looks held the same intensity she carried within her breast.

She moved on light feet around the bed to be at his back. Searching under a sleeping person's pillow was a delicate operation. If he stirred, she might be able to hide beneath the bed until he again slept soundly. Better hiding under a bed than being in them, she had always told her fellow thieves. Especially with a smelly human, though Petia had to admit this one's scent pleased her.

Cautiously, she felt for the edge of the pillow. Her hand thinned as she slipped it underneath. Leather thongs brushed her deft fingertips. The pouch rested directly under the man's curly-haired head.

She pulled back to consider her next move. Petia yelped in surprise as the man grabbed her, exploded to his knees, and faced her.

"What have we here, my Trans beauty? Come to share the wondrous lover's bed, eh? You ought to have told me of your uncontrollable passion. I would have left the door unlatched and saved you much trouble sneaking in through the window."

"Let go!" Petia tried to pull away, but Keja's strength was too much for her.

"Don't struggle, or I'll break your wrist," he said. "We don't want to wake the rest in this miserable inn. Unless it is with the moans of our mutual rapture."

"You impudent—" Petia started, but she swallowed hard, realizing her danger. Petia shook her head, deciding on another tack. "Please, sir. Please don't wake them. I was only going to take a little money, not all, sir. Just enough to get away from this awful place."

"An honest thief? Dare I admit having met one who tells the truth? No," Keja said, "it's too good to be true. You would have stolen all and left me with nothing. Not even a memory of a warmly glowing groin for my stay in this poxy inn. All we agree on is a desire to leave this blackroach-infected pit."

"Yes," Petia spat. "I want to get away from a greasy inn with a greasy landlord."

"A greasy landlord who will turn you over to the guard when I tell him this Trans serving wench is burgling the rooms of his patrons. He won't like that, I'm sure."

"You wouldn't do that, sir." Petia assumed her best fawning posture. Her mind estimated, judged, evaluated how difficult it might be to escape.

Keja's grip relaxed. "No, I wouldn't do that," he assured her.

Petia was quick to slip her wrist free. She knelt back on her haunches, distancing herself from the man. There would be no theft of the key this night. If she could convince him that it was only a desperate need of money that had prompted her venture, she might get off free. Appeal to his obvious vanity. Promise, but never deliver. That looked like the most promising course for her escape.

"There's another way besides theft, you know," Keja said.

"What's that, sir?" Petia asked naively. Inwardly, she turned cold with the too easy success. She had read this man a'right. For some reason, this bothered her.

"You might spend the night with me. In the morning, I'd see that you had enough to leave here and get far away."

Insane light flashed in Petia's cat eyes. "Damn you. I'll not give my body to anyone for money." Emotions raged out of control, emotions betraying her true feelings. Even as she acted, Petia cursed herself for it. She had intended to play the man like a fish on a line. Instead, she acted the fool. She raised her hands toward Keja's eyes and watched him edge back as her cat claws extended.

"You know there are laws against what you suggest. Trans and humans are not to mix." Petia knew this argument meant nothing—all too well she knew it.

Keja laughed. "Foolish laws that have never stopped me before. Admit it, you have some small measure of lust for me, don't you?" Keja eyed her critically. "I do for you. You are comely. Together we can . . ."

Keja dodged back as Petia's claws flashed within a hair of his dark eyes. "But if it goes against your grain, then I apologize. You miss the thrill of a lifetime, though."

"I will rip out your throat before you can lay a hand on me."

"It was only a suggestion, but a good one. I'll be gone

tomorrow. Off to make my fortune, while you, my tawny one, will still be cleaning tables in The Leather Cup. Truly, do I pity you your fate. Dirty tables and never to have shared my bed.'' Keja clucked his tongue and shook his head in mock sadness.

Petia hissed. ''You jackal.'' In one lithe movement, she rocked to her feet and backed toward the window. She held her hands ready should Keja drop his ironic pose. Petia was surprised, however, when he rose from the bed, extended his leg and literally swept the floor with his courtly bow.

''May you sleep as well as you can—without me,'' he said. His smile almost made Petia return and wipe it from his lips. She forced down her anger, gripped the gutter, then swung up to the roof.

She was more determined than ever that she would have the key. That would be little enough revenge on the smirking, self-confident human. She edged to the corner of the building and settled down as comfortably as she could. He'd not leave in the middle of the night without her knowing it. Perched like a gargoyle, Petia Darya watched through what remained of the night.

Chapter Three

Petia shivered. The night had passed slowly with no sign of movement from the inn. That jackal had probably gone back to sleep immediately. Still, it had been prudent of her to spend the night watching. It was better to take too much care than too little in the pursuit of such valuable booty.

The first pink and gray vestiges of false dawn appeared in the sky. Petia rose stiffly to her feet, joints aching from her night-long vigil. She flexed her knees and allowed the blood to circulate into her cramped legs. She looked across the rooftops of Klepht. It wasn't a bad town, but not the town for her. Quiet, sleeping, even the nightwatch absent, the prejudices against her kind also slept. It would be only a handful of minutes before people and their hatreds began stirring, no better or worse than any other human town.

Petia stretched one last time, then she climbed across the inn's roof and dropped softly down from the entrance gable. She slipped through the front door, latched it securely so the landlord could not berate her, and walked silently to the kitchen.

She busied herself removing the ashes in the cooking stove and building a fresh fire. From the root cellar, she brought a sack of potatoes and began peeling them. By the time the landlord came downstairs, a neat pile of potatoes lay in a bowl upon the counter. He found nothing to complain about, but started to anyway.

Something about the hot look Petia flashed him stayed the unwarranted criticism.

"Beginning to get the routine of it, eh?" He grumbled and waddled off to the taproom to draw his first ale of the day.

Nearly an hour passed before the inn's guests began arriving for breakfast. Petia was kept busy serving the plain breakfasts the morning cook made: porridge, scrambled eggs, a mug of ale and fresh bread this morning. Petia looked forward to her own breakfast after the night-long vigil on the roof.

Keja Tchurak came down the stairs whistling softly. He warmed himself before the fireplace, then took a table.

Petia brought him a small kettle of porridge and a jug of goat's milk.

"Good morning," he said with a cheerfulness that rankled. "A fine day blooming today. Far better than the night. Rained a goodly bit, didn't it? Wouldn't have wanted to be out in all the . . . rain and wind. Not at all."

Petia glared at him.

"Nothing like a good night's sleep to make for a good start to the day," he continued innocuously. "Hope you found a soft bed. Mine was hard. All night long."

Petia spun angrily and marched to the taproom to draw a mug of ale for him. His low chuckle mocked her all the way and firmed her resolve to separate this irritating man from his wealth.

When Keja finished eating, he left the inn singing off-key the chorus of a well-known sea ballad. A deaf woman would have heard the inn door slam behind him.

Petia found the landlord snoring behind a stack of crates in the storeroom, sleeping off his early morning ales. She threw her apron onto a table and grabbed her shawl from a hook. As she hurried out the kitchen door, she saw Keja cross the street, heading for the waterfront.

Petia ran on cat-light feet to the corner and peered around. Keja had put nearly half a street length between them. He walked purposefully, looking neither to the sides nor behind. It was not difficult to follow him unobserved.

At the docks, Petia watched as Keja talked briefly to a disreputable pair of lounging sailors. They pointed to a ship farther along the waterfront. Keja nodded and set off again.

By the time Petia found a safe spot to spy from, Keja had entered an impassioned discussion with the captain of a small coastal lugger. The captain leaned on the ship rail, punctuating his conversation by spitting over the side. Petia busied herself looking over the first boxes of fresh catch arranged alongside a warehouse opposite. Her sharp ears easily overheard the conversation.

"Neelarna, is it?" the captain said. "Ah, there's been a goodly bit of unrest there. I'm not keen a'tall on making the trip without a cargo. Waste of time. Dangerous."

"How much?" Keja called up to him, knowing full well from his earlier talks with the sailors that Captain Jelk had a full hold bound for Neelarna. "I'm willing to pay a fair rate. I don't care to be cheated, but I see your concern."

"Well, now." The captain spat again, then seemed to be doing sums in the clouds overhead. It was obviously hard work deciding how much he could cheat Keja. He grinned and named a price ten times too high.

"Done," Keja said. "When can we sail? This afternoon?"

"In a hurry, are you?" The captain's grin broadened in pleasure with himself. He had accurately appraised this one's need to be free of Klepht.

"Right. I'm off to find the Gate of Paradise. Make my fortune and find a bevy of lovely damsels." Keja did a fancy clog step.

"And I'm the ruler of the universe," the captain said scornfully. He spat, the gobbet landing only a few inches from Keja's boots. "Don't allow fools to ship aboard the *Feral*."

"Or," said Keja, "a certain lord has taken a dislike to the attentions I so graciously lavished on his daughter." The captain nodded solemnly and Keja laughed. "Or maybe I just want to visit my grandmother. Take your pick, Captain."

"Show me your money, and we'll sail on the afternoon tide," the captain called down.

Petia frowned. Keja had sounded jocular when he mentioned the Gate of Paradise, but the gold key? Could it be the gold key to the Gate of Paradise? She had always thought it more than mere legend, and this might be proof.

This was a goal worthy of Petia Darya's talents! Her mind worked furiously on the new problems involved with stealing the key. Aboard ship? Impossible. Stowing away was out of the question. On land? Yes, to Neelarna. She'd arrive in Neelarna before Keja, traveling overland. She'd be waiting for him when he sailed in. He knew where the Gate stood—he had the key, after all. She would follow him, *then* steal the key!

Petia smiled wickedly and returned to the inn. The landlord still snored noisily where she had left him.

She grabbed a flour sack and stuffed it with a flitch of bacon, a joint of beef, some potatoes and a few loaves of bread. It took only a few moments to don traveling clothes, brown homespun breeches and shirt, boots almost to the knee, a soft tam. She threw a cloak over all, buckled a short sword to her belt, slung the sack over her shoulder, and said a heartfelt farewell to The Leather Cup.

Petia reached the door, then paused. If she carried the brand of thief for stealing food, why not also for real theft? Petia went to the baking ovens and pulled out a loose brick near the floor. From the bag the landlord hid there, she emptied all twenty coins. It was more than he owed her, but far less than she deserved. Besides, he shouldn't have so carelessly let her sniff out where he stashed his money.

All continued going Petia's way. When the half-wit stableboy left for his midmorning ale, she slipped in and threw a bridle on a coastal marsh pony. He was an ugly animal, but she knew of no hardier breed of horse. She hoisted her pack onto his back, mounted and circled north around the city, then took the coast road heading east, riding as if all the hounds of Bericlere nipped at her heels.

Petia would be in Neelarna long before Keja Tchurak. The wind against her face pulled the laughter out and streamed it behind her as she rode.

The tide turned in late afternoon. Keja boarded the *Feral* a half hour before. The first mate showed him where to store his meager belongings, then left him to watch the activities as he bellowed orders to the sailors. Hawsers were loosened and shipped, and the tide carried the lugger away from the dock. Sails unfurled. The ship turned easily in the light winds and warped out of harbor.

Keja leaned over the rail and squinted into the sea breeze. He felt as if a heavy weight had been lifted from his shoulders. The guards could seek him all they wanted now—in Klepht. As quickly as he considered the guards, so did his thoughts fleetingly touch on the Trans serving wench. Keja smiled and shook his head. Why had she followed him to the port? She was no informer for l'Karm. She looked the thief to Keja, and he knew thieves.

Such a comely one. He felt a twinge of sorrow that she hadn't stowed away, that she had given up so easily on stealing the key in his pouch. Keja lightly brushed nimble fingertips over the leather pouch.

The Gate of Paradise. Such a high-sounding thing, that. And he, Keja Tchurak, thief with no peer, would be the one to loot Paradise!

Once out into the Everston Sea, the lugger coasted slowly eastward, moving as the fitful winds dictated.

Night fell and lanterns were lit. The captain came up to Keja and asked, "Share supper? Been a while since the *Feral* carried a passenger."

"You mean one willing to pay such an exorbitant fare," said Keja, with no malice in his voice.

"Your tale must rank with the best," said Captain Jelk. "I am always interested—in the Gate of Paradise."

Keja looked sharply at the captain, but the man only joked.

"I do feel a need for sustenance," admitted Keja.

Throughout the meal, Captain Jelk kept up a desultory conversation about this piece of the coast and his trips along it. Keja tried to show interest, but he didn't really care—until the captain started in on the tales he had heard of the Gate of Paradise.

"How's that again?" asked Keja.

"Mistress Mellon in Neelarna knows all about how it grants immortality," Jelk said. He scowled darkly. "You look truly interested in this."

"I don't really seek the Gate. My business involves other matters in Neelarna," Keja replied, trying to sound unconcerned. He knew he failed from the way Jelk stared.

When they had eaten their fill and a sailor had removed their plates, Jelk brought out a bottle of brandy and two glasses. "It'll help you sleep. Landlubbers have a time of it when they get out on the sea," he said.

It was evident that the old fellow could put it away. The captain filled the glasses liberally. "Drink up. There's more where this came from." Jelk waved the bottle about, inviting Keja to help himself.

Keja noted that the captain had emptied his glass,

while he had only had a couple of swallows from his own. Captain Jelk refilled his glass and sat back, staring out of the poop windows, watching the moonshine reflecting off the ship's phosphorescent wake.

Jelk sat back, his hooded eyes searching Keja's face for evidence that he was lying. He couldn't tell. "Strange story, that," he said.

"What?" Keja asked. "The Gate of Paradise?" He now regretted having mentioned it, even in jest. "I really don't know much about it. I thought it was just a children's story."

"The Gate," said Jelk, scratching himself. "The Gate to immortality opens with a lovely key."

Keja sipped at his glass. He tipped the bottle, adding a few drops of the liquor to his own glass, then filling the captain's. He had an idea that the old codger meant it to be the other way around but had forgotten about it.

"I've never heard anything about a key," Keja lied.

Jelk's tongue numbed from too much brandy. "Oh, yes. Gold key," he slurred. "Valuable all by itself, so they say. Jewel in it. Some say green, some red."

"It makes a good story," Keja said. "But only a child's tale." He wanted to say nothing more to the captain. Keja knew a good way of ending the conversation, one that never failed. Keja yawned.

The yawn became contagious, as he had known it would. Jelk yawned in response. "Tale going round that the key's somewhere along the coast," he said. "Just a tale, I suppose. You don't have it, do you?"

"Me?" Keja put his hand to his chest in mock surprise. "Never heard of the key until you told me. It's late for a landlubber like me, Captain Jelk. Thank you for your hospitality. Unless you can offer me a saucy wench for a passing diversion, I'll be off to bed." He stood and drained the last of his glass.

The captain muttered something Keja did not catch. Keja stooped and left the cabin, glad to be away, glad to have gleaned some small information from the garrulous captain.

Mistress Mellon, eh? Perhaps she not only knew of the Gate of Paradise but was also a lovely young lass who sought a lover with his astounding abilities. Keja went to sleep, that thought warming him.

Toward the evening of the third day, dark clouds began to build in the west and the winds picked up. The storm hit the following morning.

Keja stood on the deck watching waves twice as high as the *Feral* come crashing toward the ship. He braced his legs and held tightly to a rope that ran from the mast. Fear rising, he watched the frantic activity of the sailors as they scurried across the deck, fastening the hatches and removing loose gear. He muttered alternate curses and prayers for the sailors sent aloft to furl the sail—and heaved a sigh of relief that he knew nothing of such work and wouldn't be asked to help.

The captain roared at him, "You're safest where you are, Tchurak. Hang on tight."

"I don't intend to let go!" he shouted into the storm. Keja clung to the rope as wave after punishing wave swept over the deck. The ship lost steerage and wallowed dangerously in a trough. Jelk fought the wheel, willing the ship to head into the waves.

Saltwater streaming down his face, Keja caught sight of a flapping overhead. For a moment he thought he had imagined it all—no sound came—then he realized the howling wind drowned out the whip-crack of the sail.

Drowned. The word rang like a death knell in his head. He closed his eyes, but the morbid fascination of the scene forced him to look aloft again. One end of the sail, improperly cleated, had worked loose. The yardarm yawed back and forth, the wind gnawing at it. Another wave hit Keja, lifting him into the air. When he regained his feet, the yardarm was dangling, flailing dangerously against the mast.

Keja barely heard Captain Jelk shouting for someone to climb the mast and cut it loose. No one moved. None was able in the fierce winds and hammering waves.

Jelk shouted to Keja, "Take the wheel, man. Those bastards will have us all on the bottom of the sea."

Keja tried to shake his head no, but unexpected courage drove him to Jelk's side. He grasped the wheel as if it were precious ivory.

"Just hang on and don't let go," Jelk yelled in his ear. Then he vanished into the white veil of salty spray.

Keja clung to the spokes of a wheel intent on ripping itself free from his hands. His knuckles turned white with effort; his muscles strained to simply hang on. Holding the wheel steady was almost impossible.

Keja's wiry muscles came to the end of their endurance. He closed his eyes and grunted, forcing every last ounce of strength he possessed into holding the wheel. The sudden release of pressure on the wheel took him by surprise; Keja slammed painfully to his knees. The wheel swung back and chucked him under the chin—but he hung on.

Only slowly did he realize that Jelk had returned. He looked up at the mast. The yardarm had been cut away. Keja ducked his head as a wave washed over the ship, but it was not as big as previous waves. Behind him the sky was becoming lighter, and clouds scudded away behind the ship. The storm lessened in severity as they skirted the edge. The enemy was retreating.

"Stay here," Jelk commanded.

"Of course, Captain," Keja said. The wiry thief clung to the railing, unable to move. His legs had turned rubbery and refused to function. Jelk paraded around, shouting orders, getting the damaged yardarm lashed down. Finally returning to Keja, the captain glowered.

"Have to make for land. Put in if we're to get that yardarm back in place."

"You have my permission," Keja said. For an instant, he thought Jelk might toss him overboard for his impudence. "Just a figure of speech," he said hastily. Jelk still saw no humor in the comment.

With a temporary sail, Jelk worked the ship into a small cove along the coast and dropped anchor.

Keja regained use of his legs and hurriedly went below while the crew started their repairs. The black looks shot in his direction told him that the superstitious sailors somehow blamed him for their problems. Keja wasn't about to bandy words with them over the topic; all he wanted was a dry bunk and solid ground beneath his feet again. The sooner he left the *Feral,* the happier everyone would be.

He fell into his bunk, exhausted. With the first light, Keja was awakened by the rattling of the anchor chain. He heard the creaking of sails as the ship left the cove. He stirred, rolled over and tried to sleep again. Small items refused to let him be. Keja got up, sword in hand.

Almost immediately he heard the lookout cry, "It's pirates, Cap'n."

Keja's first panicked thought was to leap overboard and swim for shore. Control returned, and he chuckled ruefully. He couldn't swim.

As Keja came on deck, Jelk roared, "Break out the weapons." Keja's darting, ebony eyes caught sight of a ship's sail as it rounded the point of the cove. A pennon emblazoned with a black falcon flew from the tip of its mast. Keja watched the ship's progress with hypnotized interest. The tiny specks on the deck took on detail: armed men. Pirates. The ship came alongside.

Grappling hooks with bright silvered tips flashed in the morning light. The pirates pulled themselves up onto the railing ready to leap when the ships swung in unison.

Keja hung back and waited. He saw a sailor cut down

by a boarding pirate. Another pirate prepared to leap between the two ships. Keja lunged and caught the sailor in midair. The impact of the falling corpse knocked Keja to the deck. He struggled to escape from under the pirate's body. Barely had Keja regained his feet when another man leaped to take his place.

Keja found himself forced backward. His broken-toothed, insanely grinning opponent wielded his cutlass as if it were a toothpick. Brute force rather than any skill turned the tide against Keja. He backed away, parrying a sidewise sweep from the man. A shock ran through his wrist.

"Can't we discuss this at our leisure?" Keja asked. "Surely, there's nothing two intelligent men like ourselves can't work out." He ducked under a slash designed to separate his head from his torso. "I see one of us lacks even rudimentary intelligence."

He backed away, avoiding the pirate's graceless swings. Keja stepped inside a wild sweep and sliced down the man's sword arm with his short knife. For a moment, a look of surprise crossed the pirate's face. Then he simply ignored the cut.

"No sense, no feeling. I ought to have realized." Keja eluded another powerful cut and moved to his left as they came even with the afterdeck. He turned and ran toward the other railing, the pirate in pursuit. Leaping up onto the rail, he held a rope with one hand and turned to face his pursuer. The hulking pirate came at him with his weapon high, just as Keja had hoped. Keja judged carefully, then swung free, feet dangling over the sea. The pirate slashed, found empty air, carried through and fell over the rail. Keja swung back aboard, panting. The pirate had simply taken an unwanted bath; he would return.

The battle went against the crew of the *Feral*. The pirate leader and his men encircled Jelk and four others near the bow. The large number of dead and wounded men scattered about the deck had drained courage from the crew.

Keja let himself over the stern, feeling with his feet for the captain's cabin window. Locating it, he kicked it in. Below the window ran a small board serving as decorative trim. Keja let his feet down until he stood on it. He reached through the window, unlatched it, and dropped inside.

He moved quietly into the passageway to the foot of the companionway. The hatch cover lay back, but the hatch doors obscured his view. He crept up a few stairs. The pirate leader stood with his back to the hatch, bellowing orders.

Keja moved to the top step, then not pausing for second thoughts, burst through. He caught the pirate leader between the shoulder blades with the point of his sword. The thrust continued through the man's body. The pirate captain jerked, let out a liquid, gurgling noise and slumped to the deck.

Keja pulled his sword free, yelling, "Fight, damn you! Or do you lack the balls? I have enough for all of you!" Keja threw himself against the pirates with reckless abandon, not caring about the cuts accumulating on his body.

For a heart-stopping instant, Jelk's crew simply stood and watched. Then they burst into action. The pirates, leaderless and faced with berserk tenacity, now fought only to regain their own ship. They backed to the rail, defending themselves. Keja was everywhere, shouting like a madman, assisting, aiming strokes at any pirate already engaged. He flew to the rail and cut the ropes holding the two ships together.

The ships began drifting apart.

"Begone, you swine!" shouted Keja, brandishing his sword. Blood dripped down his hand and tickled the length of his arm. Keja stopped and stared, trying to decide if the blood was his. It wasn't. Not all of it.

Reaction set in, and Keja weakly sagged against the rail. The only time he had felt worse was after the storm. Traveling to Neelarna by ship had not been one of his better ideas.

He stared in a daze as the pirates still on the *Feral* leaped overboard, rather than trusting to their fates if they remained behind as captives.

Jelk wasted no time; he grabbed those of his crew who seemed least shaken, and set them to trimming the ship.

Keja expected some thanks for his part in fighting off the pirates. Instead, the mutterings which had been behind his back came out into the open.

"First he brings on the storm, then the pirates. The man is a jinxfish. We'd have been better off staying in Klepht."

"Cap'n says the fish looks for the Gate of Paradise. By the gods! No wonder we have poor luck. A man's supposed to live his life out, for good or bad."

All the words against him were hot, bitter. Keja was no fool. Before the crew had been sullen. Now they were threatening.

Keja Tchurak had stayed alive by quick thinking and never looking back once a decision had been made. When Captain Jelk came by, Keja spun quickly, knife driven point-deep into the man's back.

"What is this?" the captain cried.

"Be quiet," Keja snarled. Over Jelk's shoulder, he yelled to the crew, "Your captain will come to no harm if you'll just follow my directions."

For a moment, they hesitated. Then the grumbling became angry shouts and they advanced.

"Damn you all!" shouted Jelk. "Do as he says or I'll have your ears nailed to the mizzenmast!"

After Keja barked out his instructions, the crew, with obvious reluctance, put a boat over the side. Keja watched the captain climb down the rope ladder and sit at the oars, his spindly legs turning blue in the morning breeze. Keja jauntily waved good-bye to the crew and joined him.

"Row me ashore and you're free," he ordered the captain.

Jelk wheezed as he pulled at the oars. "What about the bonus you promised?" he asked between strokes.

"You're just lucky you don't have any gold on you for me to steal," Keja said. "Or do you? No? Then pull." He tapped the captain's chest with his knife tip to emphasize the message.

Chapter Four

The coast road stretched nearly empty before Petia. Farmers bringing produce had entered Klepht hours ago and no other traveler ventured out this day. The ugly pony whinnied enthusiastically as he trotted along; the sense of freedom communicated to Petia, who felt cheerful for the first time in weeks. The out-of-doors appealed to her more than the smoky, dirty human dwellings.

Within a few miles, she found a trail following a watercourse that would bring her out on the cliff tops above the coast. She dismounted and led the little pony.

Some distance behind her two men paused to fill their pipes and enjoy a leisurely smoke. "Wouldn't have thought she had so much spirit in her. Stole that pony just as easy as you please. Maybe we'll get a reward for bringing it back."

The other glanced over the bowl of his pipe. "Gonna have a little fun first, though, ain't we? I want that tawny body." They chuckled, then continued to follow Petia.

At the top of the cliff, Petia rested and let the pony breathe. She adjusted the load on its back, ran her fingers through its tangled forelock. Its shaggy coat was matted with mud and manure, offending her cat-clean nature. But there was little she could do at the moment if she wanted to make good time along the road to Neelarna. It wouldn't do for that gold key to arrive before she did.

She soon urged the pony on again, taking a rough track

through a forest of scrubby, wind-blown trees. A shiver
passed through her lithe body as she entered the miniature
forest. The tree limbs, sculpted by the wind whipping
over the cliff top, created a grotesquerie of patterns,
casting their twisted shadows onto the ground and
frightening her horse. Petia soothed the animal, cursing at
its fright even as she enjoyed the bizarre shapes dancing
about her.

The day passed in magnificent solitude, and well
before dark she found a satisfactory place to make camp
for the night. She gathered small chips of wood and
shredded some bark, then took out her flint and steel.
Soon, a small curl of smoke gave evidence of an ember
underneath. She nurtured it with soft puffs of her breath
and allowed it to grow into a full-sized fire.

The joint of beef didn't have as much meat on it as she
remembered, but there was enough for a sparse meal. She
sharpened a green branch, impaled the meat and started it
roasting. Petia leaned back, thinking as her supper
cooked. Even if she didn't get the gold key—and she
would!—simply being away from Klepht pleased her. She
felt a part of this wilderness, not the city with its filthy
humans and their filthy prejudices.

Petia delicately nibbled at the rare meat and had to
agree with Keja—the meat was tough and tasteless. She
started to toss it away when the snap of a twig alerted her
to the two men spying on her. Whether she tensed or
they had already decided to attack, she didn't know. Petia
tried to reach for her knife and make the motion seem
natural. Her hand got only halfway to the weapon when
an ear-splitting "Haieeee!" echoed through the forest and
both men charged like wounded water buffalo.

She rose in one fluid motion and flung the beef joint at
the nearest one. He flinched as it glanced off his cheek.
This gave Petia needed time to draw the knife from the
top of her soft leather boot. The men hesitated, their
surprise attack failed.

"Don't be fearing us now, little one," said the larger of the two. He kept his hands in front of him like a wrestler, groping, grabbing, never stopping for an instant.

Petia moved around the fire and leaped forward at the man. He lunged to meet her, his arms wide to wrap her in a bear hug. In one lithe movement, Petia sidestepped, flicked the knife to her right hand, slashed out. He screamed and threw callused hands up to his eyes. Petia helped him along with a kick to his kneecap. He tripped and fell headlong into the fire. Petia watched it in slow motion—the man tumbling, landing in the fire, screaming, the flames licking at his clothing.

"Wol! Wol!" the other man cried, horrified at the sight of his friend ablaze. Petia drew her short sword and lunged. The point took him in the sternum. He put his hand to his chest and seemed fascinated by the blood seeping out between his clenched fingers.

"I'm dying," he said hoarsely, face ashen. He sat down heavily, trembling like a leaf in a high wind. Petia grabbed the boot of the man in the fire and pulled him out. She shook her few supplies from the flour sack and used it to beat out the flames on his coat and trousers. The man moaned constantly, his clothes still smoldering.

Petia propped him against a scrub tree nearby, lashing his hands to a low branch. "No, no," he moaned. "Help me!"

"You'll get none from me," Petia said bitterly. She stuffed her supplies back into the sack. "You should never have attacked a Trans. But you humans are all alike, thinking you're so superior."

She threw the sack onto the pony's back, looking at the sky to see what illumination she might expect from the moon. "I don't take such attacks lightly. I ought to hang you up, then do what a real Trans would do to you."

"Wh-what's that?" The man's voice carried true terror.

"You'd be found naked, claw marks covering your chest and stomach. The tendons in the back of your legs would be severed and more than likely you'd be emasculated. See how lucky you are that I don't have the time to waste?"

"But you can't leave me here like this," the man moaned.

"Can and will." Petia wiped her weapons on some leaves and replaced them. "Tell whoever finds you—if anyone does—what you were about. Don't lie to them."

She clucked at the pony, and they moved off into the darkness, the man's shrieks following, growing weaker and weaker.

Smoke. Petia cursed. For two days she had ridden this track and now came evidence from a dozen different fires. She had hoped to avoid all further human contact after her encounter with the would-be rapists and robbers.

She sat on the cliff overlooking the encampment, watching and thinking, and warmed herself in the sun. Above in the bright azure sky a hawk soared. Its screech warned her of the boy and girl climbing toward her.

Petia considered avoiding them, then decided that she ought to be the one in control. "It's all right," she called down to them. "I won't hurt you."

The little girl was shy, but the boy acted brave. He came up to Petia. "Who are you?" he demanded arrogantly.

"My name is Petia, a traveler to Neelarna. Who are you?"

"I'm Etter. That's Milla." He pointed. "She's my sister."

"Are those your people?" Petia pointed to the smoke below.

"Aye. We're charcoalers." Petia had already guessed as much from the black and grimy hands and faces. "We come here every year," the boy continued. "Good wood."

Petia nodded.

"Are you a Trans? We've got a Trans in our camp," the boy volunteered. "Wanna come see?"

The girl stood and watched Petia silently, with nearly all of one small, grubby fist in her mouth.

"Yes, I think I'd like that." Petia pulled up the pony's stake and tucked it in the sack. "Lead the way," she said.

The charcoalers' camp was much cleaner than Petia had expected. The camp perched at the edge of the "good wood" forest. The columns of smoke she had seen came from charcoal-producing fires tended by solemn adults. Of other children, Petia saw no sign.

The children took Petia to their mother. She was a buxom woman who welcomed the Trans without a flicker of an eyebrow. "You'll stay with us the night?" she asked, and seemed to welcome it.

"If that's all right. I'd appreciate it," Petia replied.

"The children are always dragging somebody back to our camp. We've become accustomed to it. We tend to spoil them. There's so few, you see."

"I don't see many other children," Petia said. "What's become of them?"

The woman vented a sigh like a fumarole. "This is a hard life," she said, as if that explained all.

"No life is easy these days," pointed out Petia.

"Many hound us," the woman said, as if admitting to high crimes. "They buy our charcoal but revile us as they do. The young women all find it easier in the cities and the young men, well, they prefer easier labors."

Petia understood. These nomads were a dying breed.

She changed the topic. "The children said there was another Trans in camp."

"They exaggerate. One traveled with us for a while last week. A truly awful person. Always barking and yapping like a dog." Then, fearing she had insulted Petia, the woman added, "Not that we minded. The company perked up our spirits and livened the fire tales."

"A dog Trans?" Petia couldn't help but smile. "I have little love for them, myself."

"No, I reckon not." To her children, the woman called, "Find your father and the others. Tell them I'll throw out supper unless they come immediately."

The children rushed off, giggling and laughing, the only merriment in the camp. Slowly, a string of blackened men came in from the fires. One man grabbed the children by their collars and playfully dragged them off. When they returned, they were all as scrubbed clean as their natures allowed.

"Hard keeping them clean," he said. "No way to keep them as clean as the likes of you." He eyed Petia critically, almost accusingly.

"It is dirty work," Petia said, "but necessary."

"More should have that attitude." They ate in silence, others coming and picking up plates of the almost tasteless stew the woman had prepared. After eating, the men fixed pipes and smoked, smiles coming to their faces for the first time.

"Tell us a story," said Etter.

"Oh, yes, please do!" cried Milla when she saw Petia hesitate at the request.

"I'm not much of a storyteller," Petia said, but she saw that the adults gathered around were just as eager. She had eaten their food; she ought to repay them in some fashion. This seemed easy enough a way to do so.

"Do you know how the Trans came to be?"

"Yes," said Milla.

"Shut up," her brother said. "No, no we don't. Tell us!"

Petia almost laughed at the by-play. "Well, it was over two hundred years ago. The story goes that Lord Lophar of Trois Havres made an agreement with a sorceress." Petia had heard the story so many times during her childhood in her own land that she remembered it almost word for word.

"The agreement between Lophar and the sorceress Lady Cassia n'Kaan was an important one, one involving trade, treaties with other lands, contracts for shipbuilding, the transfer of livestock. Much money would be made." Petia saw she held everyone's attention, even the adults. She warmed to the telling.

"Lophar let greed get the better of him. He would have been made immensely wealthy by the treaty. There was no need for deception and deviousness. But, indeed, Lophar sought benefits beyond the contract. It is said that in his private chambers he danced with glee and that his cackling laugh could be heard all the way to the harbor.

"What followed when the Lady Cassia learned of Lophar's treachery?" Petia's voice lowered for dramatic effect. "The Trans! Never had Lady Cassia been so outraged and, some say, hurt, for she loved Lophar. Not only was Lophar to suffer, but all his people.

"With a power that not even her sister sorceresses had suspected, Cassia n'Kaan changed the human population of Lophar's demesne—every man, woman, child—into beings which were part beast, part human. A wave of her hand, *pop!* and it was done. Nor was it a simple spell. Oh, no. Some became part cow, some part pig, some part horse, and even less common animals. And some, like me, became part cat."

The children's eyes widened. Petia rushed on with the story.

"Ten generations have passed since the creation of the Trans. Gradually, most of the animal features faded, becoming human features again. Perhaps the Lady Cassia planned it that way. But the personalities of us Trans are still marked by the animal.'' Petia had them all leaning forward to hear her almost whispering voice. With a loud snarl and a hiss, she clawed at the air just inches in front of Etter's nose. The boy let out a yelp, then laughed when he saw it was only part of Petia's story.

''And that's my story,'' she said with real satisfaction.

Some of the men grunted with approval. ''Well told, stranger.''

''Do you ever get to Neelarna?'' she asked, accepting a cup of herb tea from Etter's mother. ''That's where I'm heading, and it's a new city for me.''

''Sell charcoal there once a year,'' said the children's father. ''Not a pleasant city, not for our kind.''

Petia read into that a veiled warning. If Neelarna was unpleasant for charcoalers, what would it be like for a Trans?

''Things seem to be pretty unsettled there, we've heard.''

''I'm always careful,'' Petia said, thinking about her fight with the men several days back. ''It's been a long time since I heard a story. Now it's your turn.''

''What would you like to hear?'' asked Etter.

''Do you know the one about the Gate of Paradise and the golden key?'' Petia asked guilelessly.

The simple request opened the floodgates of the charcoalers' tongues. What Petia got in the next half hour was a hodgepodge of all the stories about the Gate and the key. There were nearly as many versions as there were people around the fire. Sorting through it all, Petia decided that there was a Gate of Paradise somewhere, as she had always believed, nobody knew the location, and a person with the gold key could unlock the Gate. And behind the Gate? Immortality said some, others hotly insisted on love, immense wealth, jewels, slaves, finery, anything a heart valued.

"That makes a fine tale," Petia said when the stories wound down. "Has anyone seen the key or found the Gate?"

"No, but it's there, I know it is," one lanky, old charcoaler said. The others around the fire nodded in agreement.

"I doubt it very much," Petia lied. "It's just a good story, a tale that offers everyone in the world a chance for untold wealth—a hope and little more."

"No, it's true," another man cried. "You just ask Mistress Mellon when you get to Neelarna. She'll tell you. She knows all about it. She told me the story, and she'd not lie!"

Again everyone nodded, as if Mistress Mellon were the final authority on key and Gate. Petia tried not to show her eagerness.

"Well, now," she drawled. "Who's this Mistress Mellon?"

"A wise one," the woman seated across from Petia answered. "She knows all the herbs, and how to heal, and many fine stories, and can cast spells. You just go see her when you get to Neelarna. You ask her. She'll tell you. You tell her the Lowbend Forest charcoalers sent you."

Everyone beamed with recollections of Mistress Mellon, obviously a favorite of them all.

"How do I find this wonderful woman?" The irony was lost.

"The Cheese Ring, the Cheese Ring," the children chanted.

"What?" Puzzlement showed on Petia's face.

"Outside the city walls. You just ask anyone for Mistress Mellon at the Cheese Ring. They'll know."

Catlike, Petia only dozed all night long. Before any in the camp stirred, she rose and silently departed. Petia wanted no fuss at her leaving. As in many other ways, she shared this trait with her feline companions. Greet warmly, leave quickly.

As she rode, Petia watched the morning sun warm the vale. Dew glistened on the wildflowers, then soon dried. Under the sun's rays, wispy clouds disappeared like so many wraiths, leaving behind bright blue sky. And high above, a hawk lazily circled, looking for his breakfast.

The morning wore on, and Petia realized that the hawk still wheeled above her. She dismounted to watch it. As the bird banked, jesses flashed in the sunlight, showing this to be a trained hawk and not a wild one.

The hawk folded its wings and swooped at her. It hurtled down, the wind whistling past it. Stunned, Petia backed into the side of the pony. The raptor continued its dive, and Petia saw that it hunted her with its slashing talons. She raised her hands and let claws inch out. A hiss escaped her lips as she readied for battle.

The bird opened its wings at the last instant, as if realizing the danger it courted. It zoomed over Petia's head. Baleful eyes glared at her, and behind that deadliness, an evil intelligence. It frightened her.

At times, with other animals, she achieved some tenuous empathic contact. With the hawk she failed totally. This worried Petia even more.

She kept her eye on the sky, but the hawk did not attack again. It circled continually, shaking Petia's nerves. When the trail joined the coast road and Petia turned eastward toward Neelarna, the hawk flew north and out of sight.

"Too high," she protested. Petia stamped her foot and glared at the farmer. He sucked at his cheeks and nodded.

"Four coppers, then. For currying the beast and what feed I have. Not much around here." The farmer told the truth on this score. Petia had decided to stable her pony outside Neelarna, where it would be cheaper. An owl-eyed urchin peered at her from inside the barn. Petia guessed the boy would get the job, and his father would keep the money.

"Done," she said. "Half now, half when I return."

"Seems fair," the farmer allowed. "What's your business in the city?"

Petia tried to keep the tremors of eagerness from her voice when she said, "Looking for Mistress Mellon."

"Oh." The farmer spat. "Another one lustin' for the damn aphrodisiacs, eh?"

"Could you help me? With directions to the Cheese Ring?"

The farmer's laconic instructions would serve her well, Petia decided. She nodded to him and set off, but she had gone only a few hundred yards when the clanking of metal on metal alerted her to danger. Petia dove for cover, hiding beside the dirt road, waiting.

"Looking for a damned Trans," came the disgusted complaint. "You'd think they'd find better things for us to do. What's she done, anyway?"

A tired voice came back. "They don't ever tell us. All I know is we're lookin' for a cat Trans. Now shut up and march."

Petia went cold inside. She didn't know if they were referring to her, but a gut instinct told her they were. Only when the soldiers had passed did Petia emerge from hiding. Fear added speed to her steps now.

Petia recognized the Cheese Ring instantly when she spied it. A circle of craggy, pale gray stones eroded into contorted arches and passageways provided protection for a small hut. Hesitantly, Petia entered the Ring and, surrounded by the soft rock, felt increasingly uneasy at her unannounced intrusion. Swallowing hard, she went to the hut door and knocked.

"Come." The command rang out, sharp, crystalline.

Petia stooped and entered. A small fire fitfully burned in a shallow, rock-lined pit. Lost in the swaying shadows was a heap of a woman, her head wreathed with a shawl, the ends pulled across her face. Only her eyes glinted in the faint firelight. Petia heard her sigh.

"Ah, the cat Trans for whom everyone searches. Are you a murderess, my child?"

Petia started. "Is that what they're saying?"

"Two men slain on the cliff top outside Klepht. Lured them up there, did them in. A vicious crime."

"That's a lie!" Petia denied hotly.

"I do not doubt that. You know men. They have to make you sound dangerous, capable of deceit, cunning. Otherwise, they seem the less for it."

"They attacked me," Petia said. "The one might be dead, but the other was alive when I left him."

"Dead now, but he accused you of his murder just before he died." Cold eyes peered out at Petia. "You're no casual murderess. It's not in your eyes. But they don't ask me, do they? For pains in their elbows, and headaches, and constipation and flatulence. Oh, yes. Something for infection, something for a catarrh, something to harden their cocks, but never anything important. Now. Enough of that. What do you wish, girl?"

"I traveled with charcoalers who told of the Gate of Paradise. I didn't believe them, and they said to come see you."

"Don't lie to me, child, not to Mistress Mellon. You believed them. But they didn't know enough, isn't that right?" The old woman hunched forward to look keenly into Petia's eyes.

"Yes," she said softly.

"That's better. Here's what I don't know. I tell everyone the same. Been doing it for years. Nobody's found it yet, far's I know. I don't know where the key is.

I don't know what the treasures are. Might be wealth untold. Might be nothing. I don't know.

"Here's what I do know. The Gate is many miles north of here. A place called Hawk's Prairie. But I'll warn you. Many have come back and told me they couldn't find it."

Mistress Mellon adjusted her shawl and lowered her head. "Close the door firmly when you leave. It's going to be cold tonight."

Petia had been summarily dismissed.

Chapter Five

Giles Grimsmate leaned back, basking in the warm sun and watching the bustle along the waterfront. More days ought to be like this one, he decided. Nothing to do but feel lazy, no one to kill, no battles to fight, no forced marches. Almost of its own accord, his arthritic hand went to his pocket and pulled out the key.

Gold, no question of it. The soft metal yielded under his knife point. Virtually unalloyed gold. Three teeth, a slender shank, and the round, flat end with the peridot set in it. Runes, worn but still distinct, surrounded the small gem. Giles read them again. THE KEY TO PARADISE.

He snorted. A pretty piece of jewelry, but he had a hard time believing the story the old man had told him the previous night. Still, he had little else to do than scent this spoor a while longer. He might as well stay in Klepht and talk to Mousie again and find out more about this mysterious key.

Toward sunset the air became chill. Giles returned to The Laughing Cod, where the landlord greeted him, poured an ale for him, and gestured toward the blazing fire.

The evening started much like the previous one, the only difference being less money for wagering in the dice game.

"Ale for all," Giles cried. "I still have a few coins left." The inn's patrons gratefully accepted Giles' generosity.

Giles and the others talked until Mousie came in and took some good-natured ribbing about his gambling. "Next time, next time," he retorted and made his way to Giles' table.

The serving maid brought him an ale. He nodded his thanks. "You know what I heard today?" Mousie said, his tone secretive.

"Can't imagine," Giles replied.

"There was some fellow down on the docks seeking passage on a coaster. Said he was going looking for the Gate of Paradise. Wanted passage to Neelarna."

"Why Neelarna?" Giles asked.

"Don't know." Mousie pulled at his ale. "Anybody who goes looking for the Gate of Paradise has to be slightly crazy, anyhow," he said. "Might as well look for the Gate to Hell while you're at it."

"You don't believe the story, then?"

"Pure flotsam and jetsam."

"What about the key?" Giles fingered the key in his pouch.

Mousie threw back his head and roared. "Some rich guy heard the story and said to himself, 'Why don't I make a key like that? Then I can show it to my friends. It will give them a good laugh.' "

"Where'd you say you got it?"

"Friend of mine left it to me. He was washed overboard at the Battle of Hensaar during the Trans War. He left it in his belongings. It was booty from a raid on Glanport. Porgg didn't find it himself. He traded with another sailor for it."

Giles dropped the key onto the table. Mousie picked it up and weighed it briefly. He handed it back. "Probably about an ounce, ounce-and-a-half. When you get to a bigger town, take it to a goldsmith. Have him melt it down. That's about all it's good for, far as I'm concerned."

Giles put the key away again. "You're probably right."

Later in the evening the old man came in, and Giles motioned him over. "Care for a brandy?"

"Wouldn't mind," he said, but his eyes glinted as Giles ordered the drink.

"I've been thinking about that story you told last night," Giles said when the brandy was delivered. "Mousie doesn't think there is any such thing as the Gate. It sounds pretty fantastic to me, too."

The old man sipped at his brandy and stared into the fire. "Mebbe, mebbe not."

They sipped in silence for a long while until the old man said, "I been thinking about that key all day."

Giles stirred himself and looked questioningly at the old codger. Perhaps he had decided to talk. Giles kept quiet.

"I heard another story about the Gate. A long time ago. I'd almost forgotten it. Took all day just sittin' and thinkin' to dredge it up. That's what happens when you get old. Can't remember things. Still can't remember all of it."

Giles didn't try to fill the silence. He'd let the old man tell it in his own time.

"Up north somewhere. Kalanak, that's where it was. I was just a youngster, out to make my fortune trapping. Chelta cat, you know. Beautiful furs." He stopped again, reliving his days along the trap line.

"A trapper named Delek from the east had come to try his hand at the chelta. He hadn't done well but was appreciated for the new stories he brought with him. This was the first any had heard mention of its location.

"Delek mentioned many places, trying to give us some familiar landmark to orient on. But none of us knew any of those places. We'd never traveled there. Weird names.

"But one stuck in my mind, I guess. He said that the Gate was at a place called Hawk's Prairie. Funny thing, though. I just remembered. He said he'd been to Hawk's

Prairie and didn't see no Gate. But everybody in those parts swore that's where the Gate was."

Giles sighed. Not much information for listening to the old man's rambles but more than he had really expected. Perhaps he'd go to Hawk's Prairie. Or find the source of the key in Glanport.

The door burst open, startling Giles. With instinct born of long years in military service, he slid what money he had off the table and into his pouch for a quick departure. It took only a sidelong glance to know that the captain of the city guard had made his grand, arrogant entrance. Four guardsmen fanned out behind the gaudily uniformed peacock. The captain postured for a moment, looking over the room. He knew most in the room, many by name, the rest by sight.

He nodded to the landlord.

"Looking for someone, Captain?" the landlord asked.

"Keja Tchurak, or so he calls himself." He raised a quizzical eyebrow and gestured toward Giles.

"Not the one you want, then," the landlord said. "Name's Giles Grimsmate, or so he said."

"I'll speak with him anyway. Ale for my men."

He strutted over to Giles' table. "Mind if I sit, stranger?" He pulled out a chair and sat before Giles could reply.

Giles felt everyone in the inn watching him. He crossed his ankles on the chair next to him. "Evening, Colonel," he said, deliberately overstating the man's rank. "Something I can do for you?"

"Buy me a drink and tell me who you are."

Giles lifted a finger to order. The landlord hastily brought the ale, happy someone would pay for it. Too often the captain had lingered, the drinks coming from the landlord's meager profits.

"My name's Giles Grimsmate, Colonel." Giles studied the man, deciding what might impress the guardsman enough to make him leave. "Veteran of twenty years in the War."

"Show me your papers." The officer drained the mug in one long, noisy gulp. Giles silently ordered another.

"Up in my room. Want me to get them? Discharge papers."

"Not yet. Perhaps later," the captain said. He lifted his refilled mug and drank. "You wouldn't know Keja Tchurak, would you?" the captain asked. "Or where he might be found?"

A voice called from across the room. "There's a man named Tchurak staying at The Leather Cup, Captain."

The officer turned to face the rest of the room. "Do you take me for a fool? I know he was there. *Was* there. Where is he now?"

"What's he wanted for, Captain?" Little enough happened in Klepht. They all waited for the answer.

He raised his voice. "Seems Tchurak stole a golden key from Werlink l'Karm, after laying in the arms of his daughter." The captain waited for Giles to order still another mug of ale. Giles tired of this game, but he had played it before in other towns with petty officers bloated by self-importance. For the price of the ale, he avoided trouble. "The merchant is less upset at his daughter's loose morals than the loss of the key. He's sent his own private guard after the man. And offered a sizable reward to any other who finds this Tchurak."

At the mention of the golden key all eyes turned to Mousie, then to Giles. One started to indict Giles, only to receive a hard elbow in the ribs from the landlord; he had not forgotten who had bought most of the ale he had served—and who still owed for the night's drinking and the guard captain's share.

"Best be checking out other hiding places, men. Drink up." The captain stood. He peered down, face twisting into a parody of a man in deep thought. "You staying long?" he asked Giles.

"Be moving on soon enough. I've never been along the coast before. Much to see here."

"Be wary, then. Stay out of trouble."

The captain set his mug down, thrust out his chest, and led his men out of the inn.

A babble of voices broke out when the door closed. Giles sat back and listened to the ebb and flow of excitement. It would be prudent to leave Klepht. When wealthy merchants felt cheated, their anger knew no bounds. Whether he was this Keja Tchurak mattered little because Giles did hold a gold key. That seemed to be at the bottom of the matter and would undoubtedly cause endless trouble.

Inevitably someone would mention his key, and he'd be questioned. Simply getting rid of it solved nothing either, and Giles was damned if he'd give it back to Mousie. He had won fairly at the dice. A stranger could be thrown in gaol until the local magistrate was satisfied, which might be anything from a matter of hours to several weeks. Giles knew better ways of wasting time.

"I think I'll settle up now," he told the landlord. "I'll be leaving in the morning."

The landlord looked into his gray, weary eyes. "Yes, it might be best," he said quietly. He gazed out around the room. Giles turned in time to see eyes looking everywhere but at him.

In public he had said morning; he left immediately. The pack felt good on his back and the bright moon promised easy travel. Giles took a side street to avoid passing the city guard's barracks.

The houses dwindled away as he hurried along, and Giles soon saw the beginning of the track northward up the coast. Ahead, he sighted a man in a creaking mule cart.

Giles lengthened his stride and had gone only another hundred feet or so when two guardsmen stepped out from behind a large-boled tree beside the road.

"Hold." The guard came toward Giles. "Giles Grimsmate?"

Giles nodded.

"We've orders to search you for a golden key."

"At your pleasure." Giles gauged his chances of fighting free and saw no hope. He seethed as they spun him around and shoved him against the nepler tree, weight far forward. Giles stumbled, scraped his face against the rough bark as he fell to his knees. But as he moaned loudly, thick fingers pulled out a tiny parcel and stashed it amid the thick roots. The guardsmen jerked him to his feet and forced him to lean against the tree.

The search was thorough, but it revealed no key.

"We're taking you back to the magistrate. The captain has heard reports that you have the key. You won it at a dice game evening before last."

"Yes, I did. I gave it away. I gave . . ."

"Don't bother. Tell your story to the magistrate."

Giles shrugged, trying to remain calm. He really had nothing to worry about, yet he had seen too many injustices, both during the War and after not to chafe at this "official" theft. At worst, he would lose the key and spend a few days in gaol.

The magistrate's dwelling was near the center of Klepht. Giles bit back an angry comment when he saw the pompous jackass—it had to be the guard captain's father or uncle. The family resemblance was far too great for mere chance.

"Why did you try to escape?" the magistrate demanded without preamble.

"Escape?" said Giles, holding temper in check. "I was unaware of being officially detained."

"An investigation of the first order is in progress. No one leaves Klepht. Especially those under suspicion."

Giles said nothing. The magistrate hefted his kettle belly around and sat in the heavily padded chair behind his desk. Glaring at Giles accomplished nothing; Giles returned the stare with mirrorlike perfection.

"The key, man," the magistrate said. "Give me the key and you go free. That's all we want."

Giles wondered at the size of the reward offered by the merchant. It had to be substantial—or might only be an excuse for petty extortion. Giles had spent twenty years of his life being robbed, risking his very existence for a pittance, and took no more of it.

"I know nothing of any key belonging to this merchant," he said. "Now, may I depart? I feel the need to find fresh air."

The magistrate's face turned purple with anger. But through his incoherent sputterings, the guard managed to catch the drift. Giles found himself in gaol before the magistrate's color returned to its normal florid hue.

It was a time of waiting. Giles had plenty of practice from his war years. He lay on his matting and thought his own idle thoughts. In a week, the war of nerves ended with Giles the victor.

The magistrate seemed to have gained an extra twenty pounds in the brief week. Giles had lost half that eating the swill served in the Klepht gaol. The one thing unchanged was the magistrate's attitude. He acted as if Giles had duped him when he loudly announced, "I've received a description of this Tchurak fellow from Werlink l'Karm's men. You don't fit it."

"No more than anyone else in Klepht. Tchurak is long gone. Eluding your crack-brained men must have been easy—you spend all your effort imprisoning innocent men," Giles said.

The magistrate reddened. "You'll do well to keep a civil tongue."

"I take it ill when people deny me my freedom for no reason." He snatched his papers from his table. "I hope you get boils on your arse."

Time lost, he thought, leaving the magistrate. That the man did not again imprison Giles told him of new tactics on the official's part—the battle still played out for the key.

That impressed Giles all the more. He had thought of the key as a diversion. It now assumed a larger role in his life; if nothing else, keeping it from the magistrate and the merchant gave him a certain degree of pleasure.

Giles set off to the docks. Within a few minutes, he found a small fishing boat.

"Going north along the coast?" he yelled to the sailor on board. Giles looked back over his shoulder in time to see a man duck into a convenient doorway. As he had suspected, a guardsman followed him.

"What of it, if I am?" came the reply.

"Thought you might take a passenger. For a fee, of course." Giles saw the man's greedy eyes light up.

"Might. How far you want to go?"

"Glanport."

"Not going that far. I can take you as far as Fleth. That's about half way. You can get another boat from there."

"Done," Giles said. "When do you leave? I've got a small errand to run."

"Half hour, no later. The tide's not waitin' this day, nor am I, even for a man as generous as you."

"I'll be back." Giles stepped onto the boat and slung his pack and roll into a corner. In seconds he was on his way again, fully aware of the city guard following half a street away.

He rapidly calculated the distance to where the key and his dice winnings were hidden. How much time dared he spend in losing the guard? He set off at a rapid pace, wondering at the guardsman's conditioning. If he were as good as even half the recruits Giles had trained, there'd be trouble.

After only one long block, Giles knew he'd have no

trouble at all. He heard the guardsman gasping and wheezing loudly. Giles took a short cut through the ostler's stable, ducked into an open warehouse, then doubled back and lost the guardsman sooner than he had anticipated. He shook his head at such inefficiency. With any luck—or even more stupidity on the magistrate's part—his brief and loud inquiry at the docks might be considered a diversion not worth even a single guardsman.

The sealskin pouch lay undisturbed among the roots of the huge nepler tree.

Now, to get back to the dock without being seen, Giles said to himself. The embarrassed guard might well have spread the word by now.

With all the skill Giles had learned as a scout during the War, he returned to the waterfront. The fisherman squinted as he stepped aboard. "Right on time. Thought I had myself a pack and roll." He cast off, and they moved out into the harbor.

Giles sat on the stern, chuckling to himself. The fisherman worked at getting the boat on course and missed seeing the guard captain and four of his men jumping up and down, shouting insults and berating one another.

Glanport was much larger than Klepht. The people were busier, the inn not nearly so friendly. On the first night, Giles sat watching men silently drinking an ale brewed in the kidneys of an animal with gastric difficulties and pissed into clear glass bottles. A half bottle was all that Giles could tolerate.

He wasn't likely to get any information from this sullen group.

In the morning, alone in the inn, Giles asked the landlord, "Settle a wager for me, will you? A friend told me a tall tale about the Gate of Paradise and I—" The landlord snorted in derision and cut him off in midsentence.

"You don't look like one of them," he said.

"Them?" Giles asked.

"One of them crazy old religious folk. Thought they'd pretty much died out."

Giles laid a coin on the counter. "I'm not crazy. But tell me about them anyway."

The landlord had little to say, but Giles left the inn with nebulous directions for finding the temple.

By midafternoon Giles stood outside the Temple of Welcome and stared at it, shaking his head. It was run-down, needed whitewashing, and certainly could have used a good sweeping on the inside. A single candle glowed in front of the altar. It illuminated a large room, mostly empty. He saw where expensive pews had been removed and replaced by simple wooden chairs; even these had seen better days.

Giles peered down the center aisle. As his eyes became accustomed to the dim light, he made out the figure of a man sitting in the front row. The rattle of beads almost drowned out the litany.

He advanced slowly down the aisle, wanting neither to frighten the priest nor disturb his prayers.

The priest heard him, however, and turned a worn but patient face to Giles. He fit in well with his surroundings. "The Temple of Welcome opens its doors to you. What may I do for you?"

"I need information. About the Gate of Paradise and the golden key opening it."

"You are interested in converting, my son?"

"No!" Giles said, too sharply. His experiences with priests during the War had been such that he avoided them whenever possible.

"Ah." The priest sighed. "So few follow the Temple's faith these days. You only want to know what many seek." He sighed again, shaking his bald head. "For us the Gate is metaphorical. The seeking is the thing. We strive for a right life, a purity of heart, the utmost faith in our single god, an all-encompassing love for our fellow beings. The Gate is the promise of a more fruitful life in the hereafter rather than the reward itself."

Giles expected little else but blather from a priest. "Have you scriptures?" he asked.

"There are no copies I can let any but a true believer take away, but if you would care to look at our holy book, you can read here." The priest gestured for Giles to follow.

He led Giles past the altar to a small sacristy, where sunlight filtered down from a high window. The priest removed a leatherbound book from a ragged case of brocade and laid it on a table. Giles scooted a stool over and perched on it.

"Treat it with care," the priest requested, eyeing Giles.

"Have no worry on this score," Giles assured him. The priest silently left, returning to his devotions.

Giles turned page after page until his eyes blurred. The text had been hand-scribed, sometimes illegibly, often faint with age. It was twilight when Giles came upon a cryptic passage buried in a parable concerning travelers on the way to a market town. He did not understand at first, but Giles was intrigued by a description of an area much like one in which his troops had camped during his army days. He read it again, then sat back to envision that particular bivouac some eight years back.

Giles went back to the beginning of the passage, realization dawning on him that within the context of the teachings of an early patriarch of this church, the parable could be interpreted as directions—perhaps to the Gate of Paradise.

"Those brandies proved beneficial. The old man wasn't so far off," Giles muttered. "Hawk's Prairie, it is."

Giles worked to memorize the description when a loud noise from the nave interrupted him. Curious, he rose to investigate. In the church he saw no sign of movement, but his sharp ears detected someone attempting to move without being heard. Hand on sword, he entered the church to investigate.

Giles made his way to the front of the church, then turned to a side room. The priest lay face down on the floor, a pool of blood expanding from beneath him. Giles turned the man over and felt for some sign of life. None.

He sensed rather than saw someone behind him. The blow struck him on the side of the head. Darkness swallowed Giles as he slumped forward over the priest's corpse.

Chapter Six

Keja Tchurak stood on the sea strand, watching with some misgivings as Captain Jelk rowed back to the *Feral*. It had certainly been adventurous aboard the coast lugger. Storms and pirates. Keja snorted in disgust. He would have made better time if he had stolen a horse.

Keja climbed the twenty feet up the low sand dunes to the road. Pausing before he scrambled over to the road, he heard the tramping of feet in cadence. Keja sank back into scrubby, bethorned undergrowth, waiting. He had taken the sea route to avoid such meetings. Too many wanted his head on a spike.

The marching soldiers came even with Keja's hiding place and moved past. Keja heard angry mutterings from the men. Soldiers always groused about something. He waited until they were well past, then cautiously moved up onto the road. Keja let out a heartfelt laugh. He had the road to himself.

"I have fought jealous fathers and storms and pirates and sailors wanting to kill me, and tupped many a wench along the way, and I have arrived unscathed!" Keja laughed again. Even the long walk into Neelarna failed to dampen his spirits.

Neelarna proved a larger town than Keja expected. Somewhere in this sprawling market town he would find the Mistress Mellon mentioned by Captain Jelk. From this soothsayer, it could only be a short distance to the Gate of Paradise. How else could it be when luck rode

with him, as it did now? He took out the key stolen from
Rosaal's father and let it gleam brightly in the sun.

"My key to a greedy heart's desire," he proclaimed.

He became increasingly angry as the day wore on.
None admitted knowing Mistress Mellon. Wherever he
turned, he found only cold stares or occasionally an
amused chuckle. These irritated the short-tempered thief
more than anything else. Keja might have asked the city
guard but discretion's voice whispered in his ear that this
courted disaster. All his usual sources, the silversmiths,
the carpet merchants, the chest makers, did not know or
would not speak.

Keja thought to settle his growing disquietude with a
cup of tea. Crouched against the wall near a street
vendor, Keja warmed his hands on the mug and wondered what to do next.

"Give me a copper," came a shrill command. Keja
looked up over the rim of his mug. He saw what had to
be three of the dirtiest street urchins in all the farflung
country of Bericlere.

"What do I get for my copper?" he asked.

The question took the three urchins aback. Usually,
they groveled after some small coin tossed in the dust at
their feet or were sworn at and chased off.

Keja grinned at their confusion. "I need information.
Where do I find Mistress Mellon?" Keja held back his
thrill of triumph. These beggar children knew the woman
mentioned by the sea captain. He saw it in their faces.

The children looked from one to the other. "Why?"
asked the oldest and dirtiest of the trio.

Such boldness on their part startled him. "There is a
certain bit of . . . information I seek from her. You know
her, don't you?" It was more statement than question.

"We know her. All the dross know her."

Keja had not heard the term in many years. The truly
poor, the layer of humanity below even the dregs of

society were the dross. If Mistress Mellon catered to this class, he knew why those of higher social rank—even the lowly street vendors—refused to acknowledge her.

"It will cost you, and we make sure first that she wants to receive you. Wait here."

The three disappeared before Keja voiced his objections. He bought another tea and waited for their return. At first content to watch the parade of citizens and foreigners who passed before him, he grew more and more restless over the hour before the three appeared as silently as they had slipped away.

The eldest spoke low, eyes darting as if he expected the city guard at any instant. "Five coppers for the information, and you find your own way. This evening, after dark." The boy sounded adamant, but the jut of his chin told the true tale. Keja did not haggle. He knew the signs. He counted the five coins into a grubby palm. The directions were specific and quickly given.

One tugged at the largest one's sleeve and whispered. He nodded. To Keja, he said, "Who do we tell her is coming?"

"The name would mean little to her. Just tell her 'The Lover.' "

Keja sat cross-legged before Mistress Mellon's fire, warming his hands against the evening's chill. But the hut was stuffy, a haze of blue smoke seeking vaprous egress and not finding it.

"A lover, eh?" the old woman said. "You seek one of my potions to enhance your amorous prowess." Keja started to say that he did—the idea intrigued him—but he shook his head.

"I have no need for that."

"Such a lover, then," Mistress Mellon said sarcastically.

Keja ignored the implied insult. "I seek more. I seek the Gate of Paradise." The old woman's harsh, barking laugh irritated him. "Do you find this so ludicrous?"

"You are the second this very week seeking the Gate."

Keja looked sharply at the shapeless bundle sitting in the dark.

"Two? Another besides myself? Who might that be?"

"I ask no names. A Trans woman, part cat. A beauty, she was."

Keja sucked in his breath. The serving wench from The Leather Cup! It must be! And he had thought she was only a simple sneak thief. His admiration for her mounted.

"If anyone is foolish enough to look for the Gate, I tell them what I know. There is more to it than just a gate."

"I know." Keja's hand went to his chest, reassuring himself with the feel of the key beneath his tunic.

"Ah, do you now, lover? You know all about the Gate except where it is, eh? For that you come to Mistress Mellon. Better you should take ship for the Gentian Coast and use your thievery on the wealthy there."

"The stories say . . ."

"Yes, the stories tell of great wealth, jewels and gold, power, beautiful women and handsome men. All that is unattainable by most people, eh, lover? Don't the stories always hold out fine promises? Something to wish for, something to hope for. A magic gate for the dross to dream about. Are you a dreamer, lover? Or are you a doer?"

Keja glowered across the fire at the old woman. "I see what I want, then I act." He spat into the fire.

"Then go do, lover. Go use your clever fingers on the wealthy, eh? They will not miss it. Share some of it with the dross. Ah, but I see that is not the answer you sought."

Mistress Mellon sighed. In a monotone, she gave Keja Tchurak the same information given Petia Darya only two days before. When she finished, Keja began to fish in his pouch for some money to leave with her.

Mistress Mellon's voice crackled with sarcasm. "No, lover. If you wish, give your money to the dross. I have no need of it. I give this information to many. You're just another in a long line. Now go."

Keja started to make a smart reply, but the old woman's manner had disarmed him. He obeyed, without comment.

Near the Arlien Bridge, Keja Tchurak found a horse dealer. An hour had passed in haggling before Keja and the trader forged a deal. The horse was a beauty, black and shining, standing just fifteen hands, strong and with the look of eagles in his eye. Keja managed to get the trader to throw in a saddle, but to the horse he said, "Sorry, this is the best available," then gave his eloquent shrug. The trader glared, but the horse seemed to accept his fate.

He arranged to collect horse and saddle later and set out to purchase supplies for the journey. Clothes first, he decided.

While Keja may have had an eye for horseflesh, his tastes in clothing brought many unenlightened sniggers from both clerks and onlookers. The quality of cloth, its ability to wear well, or to hide the stains of the road never entered Keja's mind. What Keja purchased might have been useful for a social occasion and impressing the ladies.

"Perfect," said the clothier, fighting to hold back laughter. The brocade morning coat with crimson velvet collar tabs, carved bone buttons and gold piping better suited a courtier than a traveler. Keja never noticed.

"I like it," he said, admiring his reflection in a full-length mirror. The haggling over price went quickly enough; the clothier whispered to his friends that he never thought to find any foolish enough to purchase it.

Keja didn't care. He liked the way the jacket hung. For him, the line was perfect.

He found the three urchins waiting for him near the inn. "Give us a copper," demanded the eldest.

"I gave you too much yesterday," Keja replied. "I'm down to my last one." He turned up his pouch and one small copper coin fell into his palm.

"Wouldn't have any hidden on you?" The youngest peered into Keja's face, searching for any sign that Keja lied. Then the youngling asked, "You going to a masque in those funny clothes?"

The leader cuffed him. He was all business. "We're selling information, important information."

"Not a copper more."

"More's your misfortune," the urchin said. "The information's valuable." He turned to his companions. "Come on."

"Wait," Keja said, sensing their gravity.

He pulled a pair of earrings from his pouch. "These are from Lasrunal, famed for their artisans in enameling. Would they be worth your information?"

The eldest held out his hand, and Keja dumped the earrings into it. The boy inspected them with an old-young experienced eye, then tucked them into his filthy, tattered sash.

"The guard's looking for you. A special guard belonging to some rich man has come here from Klepht."

Keja was dismayed. He thought that he had evaded Werlink l'Karm's men. "Where are they now?"

"Scattered throughout the town. They have split up, two of the city guard for every one of the specials. It will be difficult for you to avoid them."

"Can you take these clothes and supplies and hide them for me?" He ducked into an alleyway and stripped off his flashy new clothing, then scribbled a note. "And take this to the horse dealer by the Arlien Bridge. Bring

horse and tack to me outside the city walls after dark.
Will you do that?''

The boys looked from one to another.

''I'll have something to give you for your efforts,''
Keja said. ''Just meet me with my things outside the
north gate. At dusk.''

The boys nodded and disappeared.

Keja collected his few belongings from his room. Had
it not been for his sword, he would not have bothered. At
the door of the inn he hesitated, caution warning him to
look before he walked out into the street.

Three guards trooped toward the inn. Keja turned and
ran for the kitchen. A startled cook and serving maid
started to protest, but he put a finger to his lips to silence
them. He turned to leave, then came back.

''How can I depart without doing this?'' he asked the
serving maid. He kissed her on the lips, as if to seal
them.

''Sir!'' she protested—but not too much.

Laughing, Keja stepped into the alleyway behind the
inn. For the moment, he was free. He intended to stay
that way.

At the end of the alley he paused, peering around the
corner. He waited until the guards entered the inn, then
sauntered into the street and headed away.

He turned a corner. Three more guards. They stood
nonchalantly, but Keja knew this was deceptive. He
backtracked to the next street, cut over three more, and
found himself getting farther from the marketplace and
the protection of numbers it offered.

Keja calmed himself, and said, ''They are mere dolts.
I am Keja Tchurak, thief without peer! I spit upon their
boots!'' The dramatic pose he assumed drew unwanted
attention. Keja bowed. One or two hesitantly applauded,
then moved on. Keja quickly joined the tiny knot moving
away and eventually reached the market.

The marketplace was not nearly as crowded as Keja

would have liked. He ducked under an awning, attracted by a young woman selling fruit. Her exotic, almond-shaped eyes dazzled him.

"I am captivated by your beauty, milady," he said, playing to her vanity. She knew those bewitching eyes were her best feature, for she had outlined them in blue.

In spite of the guards so avidly seeking him, Keja found himself utterly fascinated by the woman. He stared at her eyes, blacker than olives and as alluring. But her contemptuous smile froze him. She looked past him, signaling to three guards entering the small tent.

"Ah, my lovely darling, it has been so thrilling—and a night together might have been the stuff of legends." He grabbed a shallow brass bowl filled with a delicate yellow fruit and flung it at the guards. One piece splattered in a guard's eye. The bowl hit another of the guards on the wrist, and he yelped in pain. The third leaped for Keja.

Keja ran toward the soldier. He held out his arms and puckered up. "A kiss, my lovely?" When the guard stopped in surprise and disgust at the offer, Keja grabbed the iron rod supporting the awning, swung up and lashed out with his feet. He caught the guard in the stomach; the man went down.

Keja's weight, however, proved too much for the rod. The awning collapsed and heavy cloth enveloped him. He groped and found the young woman. "If only there were time," he muttered as his arm circled her trim waist.

He struggled and found daylight. In an instant, he was on his feet and fleeing across the marketplace. Ahead he saw a costermonger's cart and above it a beam projecting from the front of the building. Without breaking stride, he leaped to the front edge of the cart and then up to the beam. Keja used all his thief-sharpened strength to pull himself up. Looking back, Keja saw fish spilling all over the street. "Fish before swine," he sighed, seeing the guards slipping in the smelly mess. Then he grabbed the edge of the roof and pulled himself up.

He dashed across the rotted wood roof, praying that his feet wouldn't find a weak spot and go through. He jumped from building to building until he was well away from the market. The nimble thief found a secluded spot which could not be seen from the ground and rested.

His respite was brief—the guards had taken to roofs, also. No doubt the angry costermonger had told where he had gone.

Keja got to his feet and ran up the nearest slope and topped the gable. Two guards came up the other side. Keja cursed so volubly that he nearly overbalanced and slid right down into their arms.

"Stop! That's him! Stop!" yelled one guardsman.

Keja had no intention of obeying. Quickly, he righted himself and agilely danced along the roof ridge. The guards now scrambled madly to get up to the gable.

"Good day," he greeted them. The black looks might have frozen a lesser man. He waited until they had arrived puffing at the top of the pitch, then swooped down the roof, letting the momentum carry him up to the ridge of the next roof and over. Now the guards were all behind him again. He turned right and down the next valley. He was on the roof of a warehouse. A beam holding pulley equipment projected out from the front of the building. Grasping the edge of the roof, Keja let himself down carefully until his feet touched the solid beam.

"There he is." Keja heard the shout from below. He craned around to see a man in the street pointing up at him.

He heard footsteps above him, coming toward him. Keja turned agilely on the beam, and leaped to the ground fifteen feet below. He rolled nicely, came to his feet and took three quick steps toward the man who had betrayed him to the guard.

"May I one day have the opportunity to properly repay you," Keja told him. The man's frightened expression began to fade. Keja smiled, then punched the man in the stomach.

Keja ran on down the street, turned left and crossed a small footbridge. Ahead he saw a mill. He continued past, then ducked in alongside it, searching for a hiding place. The ground sloped away to a stream channeled past the mill to run the huge waterwheel. No place to hide.

Keja began to sweat, partly from his run, but mostly from growing fear. He had come too far to be caught now. He trotted downhill to the waterwheel, a huge spiderweb of a thing, but too open and airy for hiding. The guardsmen would be rounding the corner of the mill at any instant.

Keja sucked in a great lungful of air, then grabbed a spoke of the wheel as it came past him, clinging to it for dear life, letting it lift him forty feet into the air.

On either side of the great wheel a great timber fork held the axle. The main stanchions extended beyond the axle, but not nearly to the top of the wheel's arc. Keja uttered a quick prayer to Dismatis, protector of thieves, waited until the spoke had carried him nearly to the top, then dropped the several feet to the top of the stanchion, praying again that it would not be too slippery. He hit perfectly, but the timbers were wet. Keja's feet slid off, and he grabbed for the timbers with his arms. A drowning sailor couldn't cling any tighter to a mast.

Carefully, he pulled himself up until he crouched atop the cradle. He hoped that the wheel might disguise his silhouette. The soldiers rounded the corner, searching the edge of the stream, and passing down the slope to the canal below the mill.

"Can't see him anywhere."

"Maybe he went into the mill."

They trooped back around the corner and were lost to Keja's view. He breathed a sigh of relief. If he weren't spotted, it might be a good idea to stay here until nearly dark. He turned carefully to find a more comfortable position, silently congratulating himself on eluding the doltish guards.

Keja stared across at the wooden building. A short, balding man stood in an open bay of the third level of the interior. He stared back at Keja, then lifted his finger to his lips. Keja awkwardly executed a bow in the man's direction. The man disappeared, returning a half hour later.

"Those filthy barstids 'ave gone," the man called. "And begone with ye!"

"How may I thank you?"

"You canna bring back my little ones they took from me. Now be off!"

Keja wondered at the man's story. Neelarna held much misery, and Keja wanted nothing more than to be away from it as quickly as possible.

With his eyes fixed on the moving spoke, Keja leaped across the open space. His timing was good, but the wet spoke caused him to slip off and tumble into the frothy water below.

The millrace ran swift and carried Keja a hundred feet to the canal before dumping him unceremoniously over the spillway. Coming to the surface, Keja sputtered and panicked. Flailing wildly, the drowning man managed to find a tree branch. Using this for support, Keja paddled to the canal's edge. He pulled himself up and sat on the edge, shivering in the evening air and examining himself for bruises.

"I am going to have to learn to swim, if this dunking continues. This is a day I have no wish to relive," he grumbled, shaking off the water like a half-drowned dog. "Though the wench in the marketplace was a fine one." Keja sighed. Too bad she had been so quick to signal the guard. A pity what even a lovely thing like that one would do when tempted with foul reward monies.

He took a roundabout route to the northern edge of

town, twice avoiding patrols. Hiding in the shadows near
the city wall, Keja waited until the guard left the gate to
relieve himself. Quickly, he passed through the gate and
outside the city of Neelarna.

The circuitous route had wasted most of the day, but
Keja didn't mind. He was still free! Clouds obscured the
moon and the sun had set some hours earlier. Where
were those boys with his horse and supplies?

"Good sir," came the soft cry. "We have your
belongings."

"This is more like it," Keja said. He stood and stared,
anger rising when he saw not the beauty that he had
bought that morning but a long-eared mule with a sack of
oats thrown across its back.

"What's this?" Keja demanded. "Where are my horse
and supplies?"

"We sold them as our fee. These will do as well."

Keja pulled his sword. "No, they won't do at all, my
lad. On your life, they won't do."

A line of men appeared from the shadows and
encircled him. They outnumbered him and were no
starved ragtag band—and they were confident.

"Why not take everything?" he asked, bewildered.
The urchins were backed by fathers and uncles, probably
Neelarna's thieves ring. He knew the kind. Wasn't he a
thief himself?

"Mistress Mellon takes pity on you," the lad he had
dealt with said. "She says you have a good heart—and a
purse too heavy."

"No, longer," muttered Keja. He saw no way of
remedying that sad malady.

A whistle came from the dark. "Guards coming,"
someone whispered.

The boy stepped forward and thrust another sack at
Keja. Then they melted away into the darkness.

Keja peered into the sack and saw only tattered

garments. His finery had vanished, along with horse, tack and all his belongings.

"One day, urchin, when you are rich, I shall return and rob you naked!"

The sound of approaching guards lent speed to Keja. He grabbed for the reins of the mule. If the guards pursued on horses, he had no chance of escape.

The mule brayed and started off, much too slowly for Keja. The sounds of pursuit grew louder.

Chapter Seven

The farmer's boy, gasping for breath, raced up the path toward Petia.

"Whoa, slow down," Petia said, putting out her arms to stop him.

The boy collapsed. He tried to get words out. "The house . . . surrounded . . . soldiers."

Petia knelt beside the boy. "First catch your breath, then tell me." Irrational fear seized her.

They'd caught up with her. Mistress Mellon had said the guards sought her for killing the two would-be rapists. Flee! Yes, she'd have to flee. Her only regret was having to leave the pony.

The boy's breathing eased. He looked up at Petia, tears and adoration in his eyes. He had never known a Trans before and thought Petia's cat-moves beautiful.

"My father," he said. "He warned 'em. Why'd he do that?"

"Don't worry. Thank you for warning me." She gave the boy a hug, and he clung to her. Petia wanted to take him with her, but that would never work—for either of them.

"Do you know who they are?"

"Not regular guards. Fancy black and silver uniforms and they wear only a padded right glove. A . . . a crest unlike any I've seen before. I think they must be a private force."

Petia tensed all over, stunned beyond words. These

were not ordinary guardsmen. *He* had found her. Her
mouth cottony and her hands shaking, Petia fought to
regain control. After all these years, it had to be *him*!

"Where are they?" she asked, voice hardly more than
a whisper.

"Hiding at the house," the boy answered. "A couple
of them are inside, but several are outside waiting to grab
you when you come back."

"Where's my pony?"

"Down in the lower pasture. He can't get out."

"Can they see him from the house?"

"No."

"Can you get him for me? Without being seen?"

"I think so. If I can get out to the barn, I can sneak
away without them seeing. I can get him out, I'm sure I
can. And they'll never know. I can meet you down by
the stream."

Petia thought about it. "All right. You do that. I'll
wait until dark. If you run into any trouble, don't worry.
I can take care of myself, and I'll be gone by morning."

The boy looked up at her. His small face was serious.
"I'll get your pony, don't you worry."

Petia gave him another hug. "I'm counting on you,"
she said. "Now, it would be a good idea for me to find
someplace to hide until evening."

The boy pointed over the hill. "Follow downhill on the
other side. You'll come to the stream. Go upstream a
ways until you come to some big nelk trees. You can
hide up in the branches like I do. Sometimes, I spend all
day there and nobody can find me. I'll see you this
evening with your pony." He turned and walked away,
his shoulders back, head up, determination showing in
every step.

Petia retraced her footsteps up the hill, then followed
the boy's directions through the field. Upstream she
found the big trees he had described. Petia looked around
and saw no sign of pursuit. She crouched down, catlike,

then jumped. Strong legs propelled her into the lowest branches. Stretching, arching her back, Petia found a comfortable resting place amid the leafy branches.

She passed the afternoon dozing, resting, preparing herself for the flight that must come. The years. She had thought herself safe after all this time. A tear ran down her cheek. A quick move of her index finger snared the wayward droplet and flicked it away. Even after returning to Trois Havres for so many years before coming back to Bericlere, she had not won free of *him*. Petia wondered, no matter how far she ran, if she would ever be free of *him*.

Petia doubted it.

The boy arrived after supper, leading the pony by a rope.

"You're going to be in trouble for this, you know." Petia was without a bridle, but the rope the boy had brought could be shaped into a hackamore.

"I don't think so. They're not so bright, and I've got a good story to tell. I'll be all right," the boy said. Almost shyly, he asked, "How about you? Where are you going now?"

"To that, I have no good answer. Just away, as fast as I can ride." Petia heaved herself up onto the pony's back, stared down at the waif and almost broke her resolve not to ask him to accompany her.

She reached in her pouch and pulled out a crown. "You hide this well until you're grown. Don't let your father have it. Keep it to remind you of me—and the bravery and loyalty shown me this day." She handed the gold coin to the boy, ruffled his hair, and turned the pony. Petia looked back once; the boy waved.

She rode through the night, putting miles between herself and those seeking her. Petia walked the pony through the stream for a ways so they wouldn't be able to follow his tracks, doubled back often, rode across rocky stretches, did whatever she could to throw off a tracker.

The thought of *what* might be following gave her the shakes. Involuntarily, she hissed and spat, her claws inching out. Petia tried to control herself, but *he* had always affected her thus. She tried not to push the pony, but fear made her apply her heels more than she'd have done in other circumstances.

Two days later she trudged up the road leading to Becker Pass, a savage rock-cut through the Tomkos Mountain Range. The sun burned her and made the pony lathery.

When the road leveled and they entered a high, cool, grassy mountain meadow, the pony's ears twitched.

"Plenty to eat here," Petia murmured softly, scratching the animal's ears. "Time for a rest, ah, Marram? Cool off a bit." Somewhere along the way she had stopped addressing the pony as "Your Ugliness" and given him a name more to his liking. Petia placed her hands on either side of the long, thin head and concentrated.

Vague stirrings only came to her. Empathic contact was tenuous at best, and Marram had tired quickly on the long road through Becker Pass. All the pony wanted was to graze and rest. She dropped the reins of the hackamore. The pony would not wander far. As he cropped the grass, Petia slipped off her boots and massaged her feet. Never would she get used to "civilized" wear. The meadow grass was cool against them; wiggling cramped toes gave her a sample of Paradise.

The Gate of Paradise.

Petia almost purred at the thought. She had been thwarted in Neelarna by *him*. He had chased her away from the fool with the key, but Petia saw other chances to steal the key. Whatever the arrogant man's name was—Keja Something-or-other—he had to get the same information concerning the Gate's location.

Their paths would again cross, and this time Petia would hold the key. She deserved it! Memory of all *he* had done to her convinced her of that. She would steal the key from Keja, elude *him* and walk in a land of splendor!

The pony's head came up and it looked back along the road, ears up and alert.

"What is it, Marram?" Petia let her cat senses emerge. Soft on the breeze came the voices of hounds on a trail.

"No!" She held back a sob and the fear driving it. She dared waste no time now. Not now! Petia quickly slipped her boots on and stood. She ran to the pony and grabbed its reins. The baying frightened her. She knew the sound all too well.

"I hate to do this to you," Petia said, flinging herself onto the pony's back. With the reins in one hand, she whipped the pony into a gallop. His gait was uncomfortable and to an expert would have appeared unsightly, but it covered the ground rapidly.

Petia glanced back over her shoulder. Behind, she saw the pack of dogs running, heads low, muzzles to the spoor. Her spoor. Petia reached for her sword and pulled it free, urging the pony to even greater speed.

Those hellhounds were faster than Marram and gained rapidly. Petia angled for the edge of the meadow and an upward slope. She no longer hoped to outrace the hounds. All Petia sought now was protection for her back, a mound of dirt or a standing stone.

No question remained about the pack now: lurchers, intelligent dogs bred by the nomads. These belonged to Lord Ambrose, or more exactly, to his son, Segrinn.

He had found her again.

Ahead she saw a huge boulder left from some glacial age. She turned Marram toward it. The lurchers ceased their deep-throated growls and now ran silently to the kill. Petia wheeled the pony and slashed at the leader as they swept by. She missed but caught another with the sword tip, slashing its muscular shoulder.

Petia turned for the boulder and slipped from the pony's back before the pack formed for its attack. She slapped Marram on the flank and sent him on. No sense in his getting hurt. The pony trotted to where the ground began to rise, then leaped to a ledge a few feet higher than the meadow. Two lurchers followed him. Rearing on his haunches, he lashed out with powerful forefeet and caught a lurcher in the head with a hoof. The dog's skull cracked like a dropped ceramic pot. It tumbled, kicked feebly, then lay still.

Petia set her back to the stone and waited for the attack. "Dogs, why do you attack me? What have I done to you?" she called out.

The lead dog stopped, tongue lolling and sides sleek with sweat. "Trans bitch ran away. Master wants. Orders run bitch down." The voice was gutteral and almost indecipherable.

"Your master is cruel!" Petia cried. "Has he not whipped you?"

"Dog's life. Obey or be whipped. Gives us meat. Dry kennel. Bitches." Cunning eyes sized up the woman. Tiny jerks of the head and a few sharp barks formed the other lurchers in an impenetrable ring around her.

Petia's mind whirled, trying to think what might dissuade the lurchers from continuing their attack. "You can pretend that you chased me off and lost me."

"Why?" The lurcher seemed genuinely puzzled.

"Because I'm going to kill some of you if you don't."

"Cat bitch. Hate cats." He leaped at her. The others followed.

Petia was nearly caught off-guard. She stunned the attacking lurcher with a blow under the throat using her left arm, and slashed the next hound across the flank as it leaped. On her backswing, she sliced an ear from the third. This one, a lean brown-spotted lurcher, fell back, howling piteously. The dogs backed off and regrouped. The solid boulder behind her kept the attack only from the front or side. If she attacked the dogs, she'd leave herself open from the rear.

Petia drew a breath and waited for the next attack.

"Ho, come away!"

He sat nonchalantly on his stallion, grinning down on her. "Did you think we had forgotten about you so easily, my Trans beauty?"

Petia tilted her head proudly. "I prayed for your death, Segrinn."

"A noble's memory is long, especially for such a lovely indentured servant. You'll see that Lord Ambrose and his son"—Segrinn bowed mockingly from the saddle—"do not let runaways off so easily."

"Ambrose couldn't care less, Segrinn. As I remember, my lord," Petia said ironically, "lust burned brightly in your eyes whenever I was around. You never quite caught me alone, did you? Is it that failure which makes me so important?"

Segrinn's black and silver uniformed men lowered their eyes. They knew too well the excesses of their lord. A dozen serving maids had swelled with bastard children in the past year.

"Bind her," he ordered his troops. "Her tongue is sharp, but the rest of her body is as curvaceous as ever. It will be a pleasure well worth the long hunt."

Two men swung down from their mounts. Petia lunged, pinking one in the arm. The other grabbed her sword with the padded glove worn on his right hand, forcing her against the boulder. But the lurchers decided the matter. They rushed forward, snapping at Petia until she surrendered.

The men took her sword and bound her hands behind her.

Segrinn smiled wickedly down at her. "Where's that bedamned pony she was riding? Never mind, let her walk. Keep a close eye on her. We don't want my beauty wandering off, do we? Certainly not before . . . my evening's diversion."

He frowned at the dead lurcher and the other whimpering in pain. "Kill that one. I can't stand that whining." He turned his horse and looked around the meadow. "There's one missing. Collar the rest. I don't want them disturbing my pleasures."

"You'll never have any pleasure from me, Segrinn." Petia hissed and spat.

"Certainly I will. Soon."

He reached for the rope binding Petia and gave it a jerk, nearly pulled the cat Trans off her feet. "Come along, my beauty."

Petia stumbled after Segrinn's horse, acting defiant. But fear devoured her from the inside. *His* punishments were always cruel. And *he* had been thwarted for so long. . . .

Chapter Eight

The morning sun shone down from the high window, creating a shaft of light that seemed to come from the gods. Giles Grimsmate stirred, his head throbbing like a kettle drum at the spring fair. The last time he had felt this bad, he and four of his comrades had taken a weeklong furlough in a Gentian Coast bawdy house.

Giles groaned loudly and shoved himself to hands and knees. The body of the old priest lay under him, long past the point of death stiffening; putrescence had set in.

Giles turned the priest gently. From his belly protruded a knife. Several tears in the robe indicated that he had been stabbed more than once.

"Why?" Giles said softly. Staring at the dead priest made him feel years older, wearier. He blinked at the sunlight coming through a dirty pane and was reminded of the sacristy where he had examined the holy book.

"The book!" Giles got to shaky feet and stumbled through the nave to the sacristy and burst into the small room. On the table still rested the book—but with the page he had tried to memorize ripped out. Ragged edges greeted his fingers as he examined the holy book. Dizziness hit him again. He leaned forward, hands flat on the table until the giddiness passed.

"They won't get to the Gate before I do," he said. He had no idea whom he referred to, but they wouldn't beat him to the Gate! Giles rubbed the large lump on his head and winced, then looked around the small room until he found a quill pen and a pot of light blue ink. He ripped several more of the pages out of the book and began scribbling down all he remembered of the tale from the missing page.

The lines of his crabbed handwriting were a pitifully inadequate reconstruction of what he knew had been on the missing page, but he didn't stop until he had filled the margins with as much as he could remember.

As he finished, Giles heard scuffling sounds from the church. He stuffed the pages into his tunic, not caring if the ink smeared or not. His sword came from its sheath in a movement made smooth by long years of practice.

"Who's there?" Giles called. Old habits returned to him, habits he had hoped to submerge in a more peaceful existence. Giles advanced on silent feet when no answer came to his challenge. A hulking man wrapped in a faded green cloak bent over the priest's body. His fingers lightly, almost lovingly brushed the hilt of the dagger in the old man's belly.

Giles crept forward, intent on sneaking up on this unknown visitor. The thought flashed through Giles' brain that this might be the murderer, returned for whatever reason. Perhaps the page hadn't contained all the information needed, and the killer sought more.

Giles came within striking distance when a short, stained wooden club smashed down into his wrist. His sword clattered to the floor. Giles swung around, but the club moved faster. It struck him on the forehead and drove him backward. He smashed into the wall; the club landed hard atop his head. Giles fell to the floor, more dazed than aware.

Giles tried to push himself away from the floor. The pain was excruciating. He got only as far as his elbows. Then he fainted.

A knocking inside his head sounded again; a tattoo on his ribs, adding more pain to that already in his body made Giles wince and moan. The man thought he knew what it felt like to be locked in death's grip—how could it be worse than the way he felt?

He opened his eyes and croaked, "Stop it!"

"On your feet, then." The command was punctuated with another kick to the ribs.

"I would if I could. I've been clubbed."

"Of course you have. I did it."

A strong hand grabbed Giles by the arm and hoisted him to his feet. He was shoved and staggered across the floor to crash into the wall. The world still blurred around him, he sensed rather than saw that his captor took him back to the sacristy. Giles smashed hard into the table and collapsed across it. Gingerly, he reached for his head and felt the legions of lumps. When he took his hand away, he was not surprised to find blood from the new wounds on his fingers.

Those powerful hands straightened him up and spun him around. He faced a Glanport city guardsman decked out in a faded green cloak. Giles stood, weaving from side to side. He tried to will his legs to hold him and his eyes to focus. He leaned back against the table.

Some of the injury was real—the rest Giles feigned. Fingers blunted by arthritis worked to close the book of scriptures on the table behind him. He had already decided who would be the primary suspect in the priest's death: Giles Grimsmate.

"Here now, that's evidence against you," the guard said, shoving him away from the book.

"Evidence?" Giles asked. "What do you mean? It's just a book. I haven't stolen anything."

Even as he spoke, Giles heard the rattle of parchment inside his tunic. Unfortunately, the guard's hearing proved equally as acute. He ripped open Giles' tunic and grabbed the sheets.

"Bejj, Koram!" the guardsman shouted. Two more guards entered the room. They looked at the first for orders.

"Take this man to the gaol, and see that he's well secured. Charge him with murdering poor old Pater Daliferrian."

The two men seized Giles by the arms. He tried to struggle but was still too weak.

"You're charging me with the murder of that old priest? I found him dead. I got hit over the head as any fool can see, and . . ."

"And thought to rob his church." The guardsman shook the pages so hard they snapped like the cracker on a whip. "Get him out of here," the guard said. "And send someone to take care of the priest's body."

Giles rubbed his arms and stamped his feet to ward off the penetrating cold. It did little good. He eventually collapsed onto the straw mat, shivering.

When a guard passed by in the corridor, Giles yelled out, "A blanket, damn you. It's freezing in here."

"It'll get colder," the guard said, smirking. "When you're hanged and buried." He made a grotesque face and imitated a man being dropped through a hangman's trap, rope around the neck.

"Wasn't even this cold during the Pannatiree Campaign," Giles grumbled.

The guard peered in at him, expression altering. "You fought at Pannatiree?"

"More's the pity, I did," Giles said, sensing sympathy on the gaoler's part. The man was by far too young to have fought at one of the bloodiest battles of the Trans War. "Fourteen months we marched and countermarched through snow and rain. Lost all but nine in my original company."

"My father died at Pannatiree," the guard said. "So did my two uncles and my eldest brother."

"More'n twenty-three thousand went with them," Giles said grimly. Old memories were worse than the cold.

The gaoler left without another word, but a blanket mysteriously appeared about an hour later. Giles gratefully wrapped it around his quaking shoulders. It did little to fend off the dank cold, but for the first time Giles thought he might have a slim chance to convince them he was innocent of killing the priest.

Giles had no idea how long he spent in the cell. Without a window to see the passing days, he was effectively cut off from the world. Occasional meals came. He had no idea if he was being better fed than the others. He doubted it, but the guard did look in on him more frequently. Giles snorted. Probably to see if he had died yet.

But Giles Grimsmate wouldn't die. Not in a prison cell. He had lived through too much, seen too many bloody ways of dying to succumb in a filthy gaol.

He slept, he awoke in cold sweats from the evil dreams, he paced, he tried to exercise, but mostly he endured the boredom of his imprisonment. From time to time, he pulled out the gold key and examined it. The guards had somehow missed it when they searched him. How, he couldn't say.

Because of this one small lapse, the footloose wanderer was happy. That key—and what it promised—kept him sane and determined to win free of the cell.

The clank of metal weapons awoke Giles. The gaoler opened the squeaky, rusted door to his cell, and four other guardsmen dragged him to his feet. He looked questioningly at the gaoler.

"You're being taken before the magistrate," the guard said. "A word of advice. Don't antagonize him. He has a very quick temper."

The four soldiers stared curiously at the gaoler. Giles took this to mean such advice was seldom ventured.

"Thanks," was all he managed to say before being hustled along the littered corridor and up into the bright light of midday. Fresh air struck him like a fist. He sagged down, grateful for this hint that the world still existed, that he might again be a part of it.

They took him into a one-story frame building not a hundred feet from the entrance to the gaol. Giles walked on unsteady legs, but he walked proudly. He stopped in front of the low railing that separated the prisoners from the magistrate and tried to evaluate his chances.

They didn't appear any too good. The magistrate had the look about him of keeping score of victims hanged— Giles wondered if he had been given a quota that had to be filled every month. He had heard of such in other towns governed by strict lords.

The white-haired magistrate looked up from his table. "You smell, prisoner."

"No doubt, honored one. I've not bathed since the guardsmen tucked me away in your gaol."

"Murderers don't deserve any better." The words came with a hint of distaste.

"Am I already tried and convicted?" Giles asked.

The magistrate's pale eyes blazed. "Don't be impudent."

"I'm not trying to be," Giles answered, holding down his own anger. "Honored one, I was set upon in the temple, came to with a bad cut on my head, a guard kicking me in the ribs, arrested, thrown into a cell, my wound not treated, and now I seem to have been convicted already, as you call me a murderer. Forgive me, if you believe me impudent."

The magistrate continued to look Giles directly in the eye. Giles met him stare for stare. This sort of silent contest had been played out before. Giles had stonily out-eyed many an officer in his days as a sergeant. Reluctantly, the magistrate broke eye contact and looked down at the papers before him, having met his match.

"I'm told that you were found robbing the pater."

"Correction, honored one." Giles chose his words carefully. The evidence against him was highly incriminating. "I had been given permission to read from the book of scriptures. I was doing so when I heard a noise. I went to investigate and found the priest. Someone clubbed me. I staggered about in a daze. Perhaps in my confusion I put the pages into my tunic. You can see the severity of my injuries."

To that the oozing wounds on his head bore full testimony. The magistrate made a face. "That's festering," the magistrate said in obvious distaste. He gestured to a bailiff sitting along the wall. "Get a surgeon. I want that wound treated after we finish with this trial."

"Who struck you?" the magistrate asked. "Other than the guardsman during your capture?"

"I have no idea," Giles replied. "I saw the priest, examined him and was struck from behind."

"This seems to be a simple enough case. The pater of the Temple of Welcome has been killed. You are found in the church, with pages ripped from the holy book. The story you tell is flimsy, and no one is likely to testify in your behalf."

The magistrate peered at his papers, then quickly dashed off a few notes. Giles knew that he would be sentenced to die for the priest's murder and nothing could be done to change the magistrate's mind. Giles tensed aching muscles as he prepared to fight his way from the room, if he could.

The bailiff came in and hurried to the magistrate. They whispered for several minutes. The magistrate scowled, then dismissed the obsequious bailiff.

"I am now ready to pass judgment in this matter," the magistrate said. He looked as if he had bitten into a persimmon; his cheeks collapsed, and he had to force out each word. Giles sensed the guards behind him moving to thwart his escape.

"Honored one, I—"

"Silence!" The magistrate wrote another note on the page before him, then said, "It is my considered opinion that you speak the truth, that you did not slay Pater Daliferrian of the Temple of Welcome, and that you are free to leave.'' The magistrate glared at Giles, adding, "Leave immediately.''

Giles was surprised. The guards behind him were flabbergasted. One even squawked in protest. The magistrate's cold glare silenced him.

Giles bowed his head slightly. "Thank you, honored one, for your justice. Will I find my things still being cared for at the inn?''

"The gaoler, for whatever reason, has personally seen to it.'' An impatient gesture told Giles he had been permanently dismissed—and with ill grace. He started to ask the bailiff what message he had given the magistrate but found the guardsmen more than a little anxious to see him away from their normally quiet township.

Giles found leaving Glanport easier than he had anticipated. The gaoler put him onto a good deal for a horse. Although the animal had seen better days, Giles found himself liking the balky, bald-patched creature. He'd seen better days, himself.

The guardsmen accompanied him to the top of the hill overlooking the town. They said nothing, nor did Giles have much to say to them. The mystery of his sudden acquittal bore closer examination, but if such nosing about put him back in the gaol, he could live with his curiosity as he rode off in the fresh air and looked at the clouds drifting over the city. Being free again and cleared of charges made him into a new man.

He rode, a bawdy song on his lips and the golden key to Paradise in his pouch.

Above him, a hawk trailing silvered jesses wheeled in the sky, watching.

Chapter Nine

Petia Darya lay bound outside the warming perimeter of the fire. Occasionally, her stomach growled, but she was damned if she would beg. Propping herself up on one elbow, the Trans watched the men passing around a bag of wine. They had eaten, more beastlike by far than any Trans she had ever known, even the porcine Trans. They tore chunks of meat from the bone with their teeth and dipped their hands in the stew pot to grab pieces of almost raw potatoes. They offended her catlike sensibilities.

"Hungry, my beauty?"

Petia glared up at the smirking Segrinn.

"I've brought you a plate of food, but I don't think I want to unbind you. I'll feed you."

"I'd rather starve." Petia spat at him and missed.

"You don't really mean that. There, your stomach's growling. Listen to it. Oh, you're hungry, all right. You're hungry for food—like I'm hungry for your body."

"I'll kill you, Segrinn. You're a filthy swine. Your brain dangles between your legs."

"You're right, my pet. There's so little else in the world to take pleasure in."

He set the plate of food on the ground and reached for her. She hissed at him, teeth closing just a fraction of an inch from his outstretched hand.

"I'll not take you here," he said softly, eyes gleaming lustfully. "Between satin sheets, with a mattress that we can sink into as we fornicate. Not out here in the open with this offal looking on.'' He gestured toward his soldiers, one of whom sang off-key and too loudly in his drunkenness.

"We'll get you home," Segrinn continued, "give you a lovely perfumed bath and dress you in something more revealing than boots and homespun. It will be an occasion of splendor that I will remember for a lifetime. Your body next to mine, quivering with rapt passion. Much of the delight is in the anticipation, and I anticipate, oh yes, I anticipate!''

"You'll not have me. Ever. A knife in your heart is all you'll ever get from me."

"We must keep up appearances, mustn't we? Eat. I won't have you fainting from weakness. Three days travel brings us home. I really would like you to arrive without dying of starvation.''

Taking a slice of meat on the end of his knife, he offered it to her. Petia turned her head aside. The aroma of the meat proved too enticing, and she reluctantly opened her mouth. She looked away as she chewed.

Segrinn said nothing as he fed his captive, but his hands lingered on part of her body, touching lightly, obscenely. Petia felt sick to her stomach but endured. Soon, Segrinn would pay. How he would pay!

When she had finished, Segrinn stood. "That's better. There's nothing worse in bed than a scrawny woman.'' He turned and walked back to the fire. Petia spat on the ground behind him, hating herself as much as she hated him.

It was nearly three in the morning when Petia awoke. The fire still burned. The sentry tended it when he wasn't dozing. He sat on a small log, huddled against the cold at his back. He had wrapped himself in a blanket, and his head dropped forward, multiple chins resting on his chest.

Petia stretched her legs, willing the blood to circulate. She needed to relieve herself badly, but that would have to be done later. The cat Trans turned herself over, naturally as one does in sleep. She grunted once, then snored several times before letting her breathing resume normally. Through slitted eyelids she watched the sentry's head come up and look in her direction. He watched her until he decided that she still slept. He yawned, stared at the fire and decided against making the effort to put on more wood, then nodded off again.

Petia stretched her fingers and felt the claws. Her slender body became thinner, sleeker. The ropes binding her slackened. She checked the dozing figure at the fire once more.

Petia wriggled downward until the ropes binding her arms to her sides slid over her head. Her wrists were still tied, but she could now move her arms. Inching back up until the rope was hidden by her body, she pulled the blanket over her.

For several minutes, she worked at them. Petia began to perspire from the effort. The ropes had been tied well. A sudden crackling noise startled her; the guard threw another piece of wood on the fire, but he was so sleepy he never looked in her direction.

Petia let out a tiny sigh of relief. Working faster now, she got one hand free. The other quickly followed.

Petia considered cutting the sentry's throat—and going on to slay Segrinn. Feline glee rose within her breast at the idea, but the need for retribution faded and caution asserted itself. One mistake and Segrinn would have her. This time, he'd not be so gentle. At the memory of what he had done before, the woman shuddered.

Escape. She crept off, cat quiet, to find her pony.

Keja Tchurak cursed constantly, becoming more inventive with every passing mile and every additional unsettling bounce from the lurching mule. Ragged clothes flapped around his wiry frame, his blanket roll looked like a picnic lunch for moths, the sack behind nearly empty when it ought to have held riches and all his fine clothing.

Keja's discouragement grew like a weed. True, he had escaped from l'Karm's guards, but the ignominy of having new clothes, horse, saddle, and supplies stolen, then being forced to wear the rags of a beggar and ride a mule overwhelmed him. Life was not treating Keja well.

For a week, he had let the bouncing mule abuse his backside. Laughed at and scorned, Keja had learned the beggar's trade quickly. Out on the road it did not appear to be a lucrative one—he saw little enough to even steal. In the cities, he had heard that some beggars grew wealthy and fat for their efforts, but Keja had gone hungry more than once. And sometimes he had eaten food not fit for pigs.

The mule stumbled once, then began to limp. Keja climbed down, circulation returning to his hindquarters in a painful rush.

"What ails you, you miserable creature?" The mule turned and one huge brown eye peered accusingly at Keja, as if this were all his fault.

Keja picked up the animal's left front leg and examined the hoof. A stone. With his knife, he removed it. "C'mon, old thing. I'll give your back—and my backside—a rest. Over the next hill, they say. Just over the next hill, Hawk's Prairie. It's been over the next hill for three days now, eh? You wouldn't be leading me in circles, would you?"

Keja snorted in disgust. Talking to animals. He had tumbled from a lofty pinnacle when he found his only company a swaybacked mule.

He pulled on the rope and got the mule moving. Keja had gotten along with the mule, but it wasn't the same as the beautiful black that he should have been riding.

The mule continued to limp. Keja knew that he

wouldn't be riding anymore this day. Ahead he saw the
road rising into a range of hills turned purple with haze.
He was tired of the road, of working, of having to beg.
Most of all he was tired of being misdirected by peasants
too ignorant to learn even elementary geography.

And not a one of them had been the least bit
comely—or even female, for all that he could tell.

By afternoon, Keja had climbed into the hills. When
the road crested, a vast plain stretched before him.

"Oh, blessed relief," Keja said. "Hawk's Prairie! It
must be. But where lies the Gate of Paradise?" He
nudged the mule and got only a wet snort for a reply.
Keja chuckled, feeling happier than he had in weeks. The
goal wasn't far off. It couldn't be now!

By evening, he rode onto the flat. A sense of mounting
despair overwhelmed him. The plain stretched for miles,
flat and seemingly empty. The soil was sandy and littered
with small stones. A wispy brown grass grew in clumps,
fighting for its life against a hostile environment. The
mule bit off a mouthful and chewed patiently while Keja
stared across untold miles of empty plain.

A stream ran down from the hills and tentatively
skirted the edge of the barren plain. Seeing the cool
water, Keja decided to camp for the night. Tomorrow
would be soon enough to begin his search for the Gate of
Paradise.

Two days of wandering Hawk's Prairie brought Keja
near the point of desperation. The prairie was huge, flat,
monotonous, soul-defeating. He tied the mule's halter
rope to a large rock and found himself another rock to sit
on. He wiped the sweat from his face. He realized that
his teeth were clenched in frustration.

"Where is it?" he demanded of the mule. "It's not a
myth. L'Karm is not the type to believe in fantasies—and
Rosaal was convinced of the Gate's existence."

At mention of the lovely woman, Keja felt a twinge of

irritation. While she had not been a mental giant, she had been quite skilled in ways pleasing to him. It had been too long since he had found any woman, skilled or not, and it rankled.

What disgusted him even more was that he had not been wandering aimlessly and still he had not discovered the Gate. He had carefully been quartering the plain.

Nothing. Not a trace. No sign, no matter how inconsequential. Maybe it was just a legend after all. Perhaps he had wasted his time. He took the key from inside his tunic and held it in his hand, reading the curlicue runes for the hundredth time.

Keja stared across the heat-shimmered plain. Opposite him the plain ended and the hills rose with the promise of coolness. He closed his eyes against the fierce, hammering sun. For a moment, he thought he had seen the vague outline of an archway. But he had just passed by there. He opened his eyes and peered again across the all-too-empty space.

Behind the dancing curtain of heat, the image continued to waver.

Keja rose to his feet and took a few steps forward. The image of the arch did not change. Hope exploded in his chest. Not taking his eyes off the archway for fear it might prove to be a mirage and vanish if he looked away, Keja untied the mule. Pulling it behind him, he began to walk across the plain. With his free hand, he tucked the key back inside his tunic.

When he looked up again, the archway was gone.

"No!" he shouted. "Come back, come back, dammit!" Keja halted. It had been a mirage. The few steps he had taken made the arch vanish, an image conjured by tired, watery eyes.

He took the key out again and looked at it. "Maybe I should just melt it down, sell it for whatever I can get from a goldsmith." It sounded more and more attractive to him. Keja did not like the burning heat under his bootsoles and attacking the top of his head.

He glanced up and saw the archway again. He frowned, concentrating on the image, and carefully stowed the key between his belt and tunic. The Gate disappeared, leaving only the plain and the hundred-foot-tall swirling column of a dust devil. Keja reached down and rested his fingers on the edge of the key.

The archway reappeared.

He located a landmark in the hills beyond that wouldn't vanish on him, then headed for it. His hope was renewed, but he had not found real faith as yet.

Halfway across he touched the key once again, half afraid of a cruel hoax. The arch wavered, clearer now. Keja whirled about in joy. He let out a loud laugh that eventually echoed back from the hills. The mule's ears picked up at his master's antics.

"The Gate of Paradise! I've found it! I have!" Visions of lovely houris raced through his mind, courtesans serving him iced wines and popping succulent tidbits into his waiting mouth, noble ladies with an intense yearning for all he had to offer. "The Gate!"

Keja did not touch the key again until he reached the far side and tethered the mule to a scrubby tree. Closing his eyes and offering a small, heartfelt prayer, he pulled the key from his belt. He opened his eyes.

No Gate.

"Come back, Dismatis curse you, come back!" Keja lost control, pounding fists against scrubby trees and rocks and sand. He collapsed onto the ground, clenching the key in his fists. He passed beyond rage.

"What mad jester created this?" he asked, all emotion drained from him. "I'd seduce his women, steal his valuables, rob him of life itself for this if I but knew his name!"

Keja staggered to his feet and turned to go back to his

mule. The Gate stood magnificently, only fifty feet away. His jaw dropped.

He stared, transfixed. The afternoon sun blazed down on two immense white Gentian marble columns joined at the top with an ornate arch wrought of a delicately veined black stone and shot through with red. Keja walked to the Gate and touched one glossy, cool column.

"It wasn't a fool's chase. It was real!" He stood back and stared at the arch. Large runes across the top boldly proclaimed: THE GATE OF PARADISE. Puzzling out the smaller inscription required too much effort. Keja vowed to study it at length. Later.

Between the two columns stretched an iron gate decorated with complex, swirling branches and delicate leaves. At the center where the two gates met and well within the reach of a person's grasp were five hasps, one above the other, each with a lock.

Keja looked at the key in his hand. "The Gate of Paradise," he whispered. He stepped forward and fitted the key into the bottom lock. He turned it, but it refused to budge. Keja pulled the key out and examined the lock closely. He saw not the least sign of weakening rust, and the internal mechanism had been cunningly concealed behind a thick plate.

"It bears closer examination," he said, "later." Keja pulled the key from the lock and tried it in the next keyhole. His key failed to open the second lock, and the third. When he tried the fourth lock, almost in desperation, Keja felt the tumblers give and the shank of the lock fell away. Keja opened the hasp and let the opened lock dangle from the staple. The fifth lock would not open, either.

Keja frowned, trying to understand the mind of whoever had constructed the Gate. Long ago he had discovered a thief's work became much easier if he placed himself in the victim's head and tried to *understand*.

Nothing came. "Never mind," he said aloud. "I've

found the Gate. Locks have never stopped me before.''
Confidently, Keja rummaged in his pouch until he found
a small ring of slender picks.

For the next half hour, Keja worked at picking the four
locks not opened by his key. He used every pick on
every lock without success. Frustrated, he began again,
summoning skills taught him by the greatest thieves in all
of Bericlere. Sweat beaded on his forehead and ran into
his eyes. His face contorted in intense concentration. At
times, his tongue would slip out from between his teeth
and twist as if he thought this would add some extra
dimension to the work at hand.

Again, he used all the picks against the four stubborn
locks. Finally, he stepped back, gave the gate a good
kick, and turned to stalk away.

"Not having any success?"

The man sat astride his horse, watching with quiet
amusement.

Keja grabbed for his sword, then reason regained
control. Without the key in his hand, Keja had been
unable to see the Gate. Therefore, the cool and collected
rider could see nothing of the Gate. It had to work that
way. Keja relaxed, his mind turning to the lie he would
tell.

"Just angry because I have to cross this desolate
plain," Keja answered.

"Yes, I imagine so," the stranger said. He looked
across the flat, barren expanse. "It is a wide one, all
right. I see from your animal's tracks that you've just
come from the other side of the hills. Now you have to
go back, eh?"

"I do, if it's any matter to you." Keja grabbed at the
excuse.

"You couldn't get the other four locks open?"

"No, only the one." It took only a second, then Keja
blanched. He had answered the casual question without
thinking and given away all! "What locks?"

Giles Grimsmate quietly held up his gold key.

Keja's hand flashed to his side. The key still rested there, tucked firmly in his belt. "Where did you get that?" he demanded.

"I might ask the same of you, except that I know about l'Karm. I had troubles of my own with his guard—they mistook me for you." Giles dropped his reins and dismounted.

Keja watched as the older man walked to the Gate and fitted his key into the bottom lock. It would not open, nor did the next. The third lock snicked open easily. The fourth lock was hanging open. The topmost lock would not budge for Giles' key.

"This is something of a puzzle," Giles said. "We'll try again later. Dealing with magicks can be tricky—not something I cherish doing. It might be that they will only unlock at a certain time. I'm going to camp up there." He waved up the hillside to a flat space shaded by stunted nepler trees. "Care to join me?"

"I've nothing to offer for food," Keja said.

"No matter. Come on." Giles picked up the reins of his horse and started for the dubious shelter of the trees.

Keja watched him with a puzzled look. Then he untied his mule and followed.

Giles unsaddled his horse and handed the reins to Keja. "Tether the animals while I gather firewood."

"You trust me with your horse?" Keja asked, startled. The animal, as old and decrepit as it was, looked far better than his mule.

Giles laughed. "No, not much. But you're not going anywhere until the Gate is open. Nor am I. So a tiny bit of trust, maybe."

Keja shook his head. "You're a rare one." He did as Giles asked and, soon enough, a wisp of smoke grew into flame, then bloomed into a welcome fire. The meal was not fancy, but to Keja it represented a banquet. When he had finished, Giles offered him a pipe. Keja waved it off.

Giles filled it for himself and lay back on an elbow to enjoy the pungent tobacco mix.

"Were you here long before I arrived?" Giles asked between puffs.

"No." Keja wondered how much the man knew and how much he ought to tell him. "I found the Gate, unlocked the one lock and tried to pick the others. You certainly startled me."

"You were concentrating so hard that you didn't hear me come up," Giles said. "You should have seen the look on your face."

Keja bristled at this, then calmed. "You obviously know where I got my key. How'd you come by yours?"

"Won it in a dice game. The sailor who wagered it didn't know anything about the Gate, but another knew quite a bit about it. He told me the story in exchange for enough brandy to float a brigantine."

Little by little, the two men relaxed. Talk became easier as Giles told of his time in the War and his restless need to wander. Keja warmed to the telling and regaled Giles with some of his more successful exploits.

Giles thought that perhaps he bragged too much. Still, this Keja Tchurak looked like a man who could handle himself in a spot of trouble. Giles knew Keja spoke the truth about being a thief; only a thief could be conned into trusting a street urchin. Giles had long ago learned that those capable of theft were the ones most easily robbed. They never thought it could happen to them—and so it did.

The moon rose, nearly full. Giles tapped the dottle from his pipe and unrolled his blankets. "We'll see what the morning brings. Better luck, perhaps."

"Hm?" Keja was deep in his own thoughts. "Oh, yes. Good night." He fetched his own ragged roll and stretched out near the fire. Soon both men slept.

Petia crept along the hillside's contour. She had left

Marram tied to a tree downwind, over a mile distant. Petia had watched the two men for nearly five hours, trying to understand what transpired between them.

It was a bizarre ritual they went through. She watched the stranger guide his horse down the hillside and sit quietly watching whatever Keja was about. She was bemused when Keja drew back his foot and aimed a kick at empty air.

Whatever they did, they had finally given up and made camp. Petia chewed on dried meat from her pouch while she watched the men being domestic. When they were soundly asleep, she would act.

Keja still had the gold key. Petia had seen it glint in the sunlight. She was determined to have it. For all she had been through, it was small enough compensation.

The moonlight proved enough for her acute night vision to find a quiet path into the campsite. She squatted down and watched the two men's chests rise and fall. Both slept soundly. The fire burned lower and neither rose to tend it. That was a good sign.

In another half hour, Petia decided to make her move. She stealthily moved down the hill toward the men. The stranger slept on one side of the fire and Keja on the other. She went to Keja.

A loud snap made her jump. A limb, burned through, fell into the flames, scattering sparks into the velvet black of the night sky. Both men burst from their blankets and pinned her in seconds. Petia fought with all the skill imparted by her cat nature, but she was no match for such strong men.

Keja locked one of her arms behind her. Petia snarled in pain, then stopped fighting. He would relax; her chance for escape would come if she waited.

"Look who we have here." Keja grinned at Petia.

Giles glanced at him. "You know that Trans?"

"You've not met, have you? A serving maid from The Leather Cup in Klepht. She tried to steal the key from me once before. The gods alone know how she comes to be here.'' Keja yawned. ''Let's tie her up and sort this out in the morning. I'm still tired from my trip. But do watch her. She's a tough one.''

Giles fetched rope from his pack. The two men tied Petia hand and foot and laid her none too gently near the fire. Keja slipped quickly back to sleep, but Giles lay awake watching. He wondered where this young Trans fit into this.

Chapter Ten

Giles Grimsmate came awake instantly, too many clues assailing his senses. He rolled over to check their prisoner. Gone. Giles jerked erect, grabbed at his weapons, and yelled at Keja, "She's escaped!"

"Yes, I have." Giles spun about, feet tangling in his blanket. Petia squatted on the opposite side of the fire. "I thought I'd fix some breakfast. Porridge?"

Giles rolled out of his blankets and stood, running his fingers through his black, gray-shot hair. "Bedamned," he said. "How did you get out of those ropes? I tie a fair knot, and those have held stronger ones than you."

Petia smiled wickedly, teeth showing. "It's a little trick of mine." She walked over to Keja's sleeping figure and kicked him none too gently. "Up, you lazy lout. The day's half gone."

Keja groaned and blinked. He closed his eyes again and muttered, "I was dreaming that the serving wench had got free."

"Listen to him." Petia returned to the fire and ladled porridge into bowls, then handed one to Giles. "I'm Petia Darya. And you?"

Giles admired her straightforwardness. "Giles Grimsmate," he replied. "My pleasure. What were you looking for last night?"

"His key, of course," she said. "I've completely lost my touch, I guess. That's the second time I've failed."

Giles nodded. "You just tackled a pair of men whose

117

senses are extra sharp, honed by years of suspicion. Twenty years of the War did that to me. I don't know about Keja. Maybe thievery does that to you."

"It does. But I'm obviously out of practice."

Keja muttered and groaned for a half hour, prowling around the campsite, bowl and spoon in hand. Finally, Giles tired of inaction and said, "Let's try the keys again."

"More than one?" Petia asked, her sharp eyes darting from one man to the other. Giles felt undercurrents of greed rising in her. If one key was valuable enough to chase after, two made the hunt twice as rewarding.

"We each have one." Giles warily studied the Trans.

"Maybe I should have tried to steal yours instead." She caught Giles' dark look. "And maybe it's just as well I didn't."

Giles headed toward the Gate, holding the glittering gold key between thumb and forefinger.

"How do you know where the Gate is?" Petia asked.

"You can't see it?" Giles held out his hand. "Try the key."

Petia daintily touched her finger to the key. The Gate suddenly shimmered below at the edge of the plain.

Keja came stumbling down the path behind them. "Is it still there? It didn't go away, did it? I find it so tiring to deal with magicks of this order."

Giles raised his eyes to the heavens. "Open your eyes, man. No, it didn't go away." He walked to the Gate and inserted his key into the lowest lock. Trying each in turn, he found that his key once again opened only the third lock. "Might require opening in a particular sequence," he muttered.

Petia stood back and watched the seeming charade of Giles trying a different order in what she saw only as empty air. She became bored and wandered off. Keja sat on the ground, his head in his hand, still trying to wake up completely.

"Did you see that, Giles?" he yelled. "She walked through that stone column."

Giles looked up from his work. He saw Petia on the other side of the Gate. "What's over there?" he yelled to her.

"You don't have to shout. I hear perfectly fine, extraordinarily well, in fact. Nothing's over here, except the plain." She turned and gestured behind her across the barren land.

"Come back here for a minute."

Petia strolled back, walking "through" the metal bars of the Gate, and stood at Giles' side.

"Great Ephrem! They're illusory," Giles cried.

"What?"

"The gate, the columns, the entire Gate of Paradise. You walked away from me and *through* the stone columns. You've returned by walking *through* the bars." A slow smile crossed Giles' face. "We're home free."

Giles briskly strode forward and smashed hard into the Gate. He reeled back and fell, while Petia walked forward and *through* the Gate, unimpeded.

Giles stared up, a foolish expression on his face. He looked from Petia to the key in his hand to the Gate.

"Mind explaining this?" asked Petia. "Why did you fall?"

"I thought to simply walk through the Gate, as you just did. But while I hold the key, the Gate is solid, impassable."

Petia rejoined him, sticking out her hand. "Let me hold it."

Reluctantly, Giles passed over the key. He rose; the Gate had vanished totally. When he walked forward, he felt only hot breeze against his flesh. Giles looked back and saw Petia's expression—to her, as long as she held the key, he passed *through* the solid Gate.

"I thought it would work," he said sadly. "I thought I

might enter, but when I hold the key, the Gate is impenetrable.''

''And,'' cut in Keja, ''when you no longer hold the key, you can't see the Gate at all, so traverse the distance with no resistance.''

Giles took the key back from Petia, who surrendered it to him with obvious regrets. He saw the light in her eyes die as the Gate vanished for her and reappeared to him. Giles went to the Gate, closed his eyes and stepped forward. He smashed into solid metal.

''You tried that,'' pointed out Petia. ''Why did you try it again?''

''Something Keja said. I thought if I didn't see the Gate but still held the key . . .'' Giles' voice trailed off. It sounded lame, silly. Like so much else in his life, it hadn't worked out the way he'd intended.

''I'm going to make one more attempt to pick those locks,'' Keja said. ''I've come too far, and endured such great hardships, to give up easily. Besides, the challenge excites me.''

''A knothole excites you,'' muttered Petia. Keja gave her a superior look, then set to work picking the locks.

Finally Keja gave up. ''I don't understand it at all. There's supposed to be immense wealth behind the Gate of Paradise. You don't suppose it's a false gate, do you?''

''No,'' Giles said. ''The story of the Gate mentions only the one.''

Keja's head drooped. ''My bad luck with the locks is exceeded only by the dismal luck I've had recently with women and retaining my belongings.''

''The picks did nothing?'' Giles eyed the Gate. No amount of explosive would budge it, either, he guessed. Physical against magical proved an unequal matching; the magicks usually triumphed.

''Not even a scratch was left,'' Keja said. ''And it

isn't my lack of ability. Those locks were not meant to be picked. Not even by the masters.''

"It's obvious, then, how to open the Gate." Petia smiled sweetly at the two men staring at her.

As much as her superior nature irritated him, Giles liked the imp lurking in those eyes. "All right, brilliant one. I knew you showed up for a purpose. Reveal all to your humble audience.''

"It's as plain as a hump on a lirjan. There are five locks and you've opened two of them with two keys. There are three more keys somewhere.''

Giles said nothing, digesting Petia's words. He had felt alive in this quest. The tiredness descended upon him once more, making him into a man years older than his age.

"That ends it," he said. "We've only got two keys, and Keja hasn't been successful in picking the other locks, so we're out of luck." He stared at the Gate of Paradise. "It would have been the adventure of a lifetime," he said softly.

"You don't suppose we could find the other three keys, do you?" Petia looked from Giles to Keja and back. "You give up too easily.''

The men stared at her.

"Well, is it such a crazy idea? Find three keys and the fortune is ours.''

Giles gazed off toward the Gate. "The idea is sound, but I have no hint where to go a'hunting for the other keys.''

"What do we have to lose?" the Trans insisted.

Keja looked up and scowled. "You mean form a team to go searching for them? Why should I become partners with a Trans who tries to steal my key from me, not once, but twice?''

"What bothers you most, Keja? The fact that I'm a Trans, or a female, or a more clever thief than you?''

Petia threw a clump of dirt at Keja. "Back in Klepht it didn't matter that I was Trans."

"No, it didn't," Keja said, a slow smile crossing his lips. "Still doesn't. But you are hardly the more clever thief. Let me tell you of . . ."

Giles broke in. "It hardly matters. None of us knows where to find—or steal—the other three keys. Even if we did, I can't say I trust either of you. In the army we executed thieves, and I did my share of that chore with a certain willingness." Giles heaved a gusty sigh. "And you two obviously don't trust each other. We wouldn't make a very successful team, it appears to me."

"We might, once we got to know each other." Petia's eyes glinted. "You both smell nice. And I don't have anything better to do. There's a troop of guards after me claiming I killed a couple of men outside Klepht. It was self-defense, I swear it was." Neither Giles nor Keja much cared about this. They had experienced similar problems of their own. "There's worse," Petia went on. "A despicable insect named Segrinn also follows me. I was indentured to his father, Lord Ambrose. I ran away to escape Segrinn's bed."

"You do that a lot, don't you?" Keja asked.

"Never mind," cut in Giles, irritated at all that had happened that day. "What's the point to this, Petia?"

"I'll be frank. I wouldn't mind the protection you two could give me." She curled up, catlike, and watched their responses. Petia continued, "Keja has guards after him, too. His key is stolen, if I heard right back in Klepht."

Giles nodded. "They came into The Laughing Cod the night after I won the key. City guards and guards of someone named l'Karm."

"They almost caught me in Neelarna," Keja said morosely. "I'm sure they're still after me. Sooner or later, they'll pick up the trail."

"And you, Giles?" Petia smiled sweetly. "Who is after you?"

Giles picked up a stick and drew squares and circles in the dirt at his feet. "Demons," he answered. Demons left over from a futile war, from killing too many men like himself foolishly loyal to self-serving commanders, from losing wife and sons, from knife-edged memories chasing him across the barren lands locked within his head.

Giles said, "You know, I spent an afternoon in a temple in Glanport reading from a holy book."

"Religion? You don't look the type." Keja glared at him, as if expecting better.

"Listen up." The crack of Giles' command silenced the wiry thief. "I sought clues to this gate. The Temple of Welcome is an old religion, dying. I skimmed their scriptures.

"At the beginning was a passage that mentioned keys. It wasn't what I sought so I skimmed on. Something about five tribes closely connected at the beginning of time. The five tribal leaders said the keys were given to them by the gods. Probably had the keys made and concocted the story. But it welded the tribes together into a true nation."

"Politics and religion, always the perfect combination for keeping people in line," grumbled Keja. Giles ignored him and went on with his tale.

"Their world grew cold and they had to move.

"So Petia may well be right. Five keys. But we don't know where the other three are."

Petia spoke so softly Giles almost missed her words.

"I think I know where another of the keys is."

Giles motioned for her to continue.

"I come from Trois Havres, across the Everston Sea, on the continent of Milbante. Trois Havres are the three richest coastal cities. Living somewhere inland is a sorceress—the Flame Sorceress. There are many stories about her, but one I remember from my childhood involves a gold key.''

Petia stopped.

Keja broke the silence. ''You're suggesting that we all go looking for the third key? Not this lad. Keja Tchurak is a loner. I work best alone—or perhaps with a willing woman beside me. In bed.'' He glared at Giles and Petia, as if daring them to dispute his claims.

''For my part,'' said Giles, ''I'm wandering nowhere in particular, but I don't need the sort of adventure you're suggesting.''

Petia shrugged. ''It was just a thought. A bit selfish on my part. I'd like to see my home again.''

''It would be a fantastic adventure, though, wouldn't it?'' Keja mused. ''Just think—gather the five keys, open the Gate, rake in the immense wealth. What a great story to tell my grandchildren, of which there will be legions.'' He pursed his lips and lost himself in consideration of this wild scheme.

''Two thieves and an old warrior,'' Giles said, ''off to seek their fortunes. It sounds like a tale told by a drunken sailor. Let me be honest with you. How could we ever trust one another?''

''Are you so pure, Giles?'' asked Keja. ''Have you never stolen? Even a crumb or two when you were hungry?''

''That was different,'' Giles said, defensive. ''My men starved and . . .''

''Aha, you admit it then. Theft is theft, my friend.'' Keja smirked. ''Me. I'm for trying. Come with us, Giles. We need your experience—and you might make upright citizens of Petia and me. You've got nothing else to do, you admit that.''

Giles looked at the two. For all the jesting tone, Keja's eyes were sincere. Petia nodded solemnly.

''I will regret this. I know it.'' He rose. ''Let's take

one more look at the Gate." He examined the archway once more.

THE GATE OF PARADISE in large runic letters blazed out at Giles. Then he worked to decipher the smaller, less distinct runes. They read: ONLY ONE MAY ENTER.

Short and direct, Giles thought, but cryptic. Did it mean that only one may enter at a time or that only one may ever enter? Giles decided to keep this small secret to himself.

"The journey might be worth it," Giles said aloud. Petia and Keja came over.

"So we go to Trois Havres to find this Flame Sorceress?" asked Keja. "Petia tells me she is reputed to be gorgeous, just the sort of woman who is irresistibly attracted to me." Before Petia said a word, Keja clamped one hand over his heart and cried, "But I will forsake this sorceress if only you, my darling, will—"

"Enought of this," cut in Giles. "I have misgivings enough about my decision to join in this mad search for what might not exist." He thought of the dead priest. The pater had said the Temple of Welcome taught that the seeking was more important than the finding. Giles began to think such a teaching carried with it a kernel of truth. Again, with just the promise of a goal, no matter how tenuous, Giles felt himself coming alive and wanting to travel, to experience, to see what the world had to offer.

Keys or not, entry through the Gate or not, he would seek. The finding might be nothing or it might represent more. Only the attempt would tell the truth.

Petia's head came up. "Shh," she said, putting her fingers to her lips. She listened intently.

"What is it?" asked Keja. "Do you listen for the rapturous beating of my heart? With you so near, I can do nothing else but feel the heat, the excitement, the—"

"Keja!" Giles' sharp command silenced the wiry thief. "Still your tongue and use your ears. Listen, man!"

"There it is again," said Petia, her face set into a mask of fear. "Segrinn's on my trail again."

"What is it? What do you hear?" Giles asked.

"You don't hear it yet? No, you wouldn't. My hearing is superior because of my cat nature. Segrinn's lurchers bay, hot on my spoor. They're still in the distance. We'd better leave. Soon."

Without questioning her further, Giles turned and trotted up the trail to the camp. Keja and Petia followed. When they caught up with the grizzled old warrior, Giles had already kicked dirt on the fire. Petia threw her belongings into her sack and strapped it to Marram's back.

Giles glanced at Keja. "Hurry, man. Lurchers are no respecter of life. Get a move on."

"Do they truly send *lurchers* after her?" Keja asked. "That seems dubious to me. They are expensive beasts, and cantankerous. Their very nature, their intelligence, make them of questionable use."

"If we are to find the keys, we must survive," said Giles. "And to survive means depending on one another. My ears do not pick up the sounds Petia's do. . . ." Giles left the rest of the sentence dangling. Keja understood. His senses weren't as acute as the Trans woman's, either.

"Mistake pulling out so precipitously," he grumbled. Quickly, they packed and saddled the animals. Petia, impatient, was the first to swing up into her saddle.

Giles stood gazing around the campsite, wishing they had time to obliterate all evidence that three people had camped here. Segrinn and his men might be put off their trail. Giles shook his head sadly, realizing how wrong he was. Lurchers were not easily fooled.

"Did you check the locks?" he asked Keja.

"No, I didn't think to."

"Start on up the trail into the hills. I'll catch up." Giles kicked his ancient horse into a trot toward the Gate of Paradise, pulling his key free so that he could see. He cursed. The lock for Keja's key dangled open. Without dismounting, Giles reached over and snapped it closed. For good measure, he tried the other four locks. All secure.

The horse surprised him with the heart it displayed in its valiant uphill ride. He caught up with the other two quicker than he'd anticipated. He slowed to a walk. "Got your key?" he asked Keja. Giles saw that he would lend more than experience to this strange partnership; he would have to nursemaid the other two constantly or all their heads would be spitted and put out in the sun.

Keja patted his chest. Giles curtly acknowledged as the thief put the string with his key around his neck and tucked it into his tunic front.

"Trusting souls, aren't we? Shall we pick up the pace and see if we can put some distance between us and this Segrinn that Petia talks about with such loathing? I don't like him and I've never even seen him. At the moment, I don't like anyone who travels with a force of men. They are too likely to seek the reward on my head—or be the pawns of a jealous husband or father."

Giles scowled. Keja appeared to enjoy this. Giles urged his mount to the front. "I've been over this trail. Let me know if you can't keep up." We must make a funny-looking bunch, he thought. A horse, a marsh pony, and a mule; a has-been warrior, a Trans woman, and a thief dressed as a beggar.

Giles Grimsmate then thought only of eluding their pursuers. *Their* pursuers, he told himself, not just Petia's.

Segrinn sat astride his horse, directing his men. The lurchers milled about, yelping at the occasional scent of their quarry but confused with the other spoor mingling with that of the cat woman.

"What's the matter with those dogs?" he shouted. "Whip them into finding the trail."

"They seem confused, Lord," a soldier shouted back to him. "There are footprints and hoofprints all around this area, ones not belonging to a Trans."

Segrinn rode along the edge of the plain until he reached the place where many footprints and a set of hoofprints led across the ground. He guided his horse alongside the tracks until they came to the place where Petia, Giles, and Keja had attempted to unlock the Gate of Paradise earlier that day.

"There's nothing here, you idiots. She laid false trail to confuse us. It won't work with me!" Segrinn shouted. "Scout around the area, then report what you find."

The evidence of three people camping and remnants of a recent fire did little to improve Segrinn's mood. They had let the Trans woman get away when he had thought they were close on her trail. Now the lurchers seemed confused. Where he expected to find one person, three now left their debris.

"Chain the dogs. We'll camp here for the night. We can't be far behind the Trans now, no thanks to following the wrong trail for so long. She'll be mine yet." Segrinn slid from his horse, and paced back and forth, rubbing his hands together. "Get a fire built. Start a meal. Must I tell you every move to make? Damn!"

Is Petia Darya worth this effort? Segrinn wondered. Scores of women on the estate would be happy to oblige even his most outrageous whim. But Segrinn refused to quit. The damned Trans had become an obsession.

Chapter Eleven

"This is what I was looking for." Giles reined in and waited for the others. Keja's mule obstinately balked, forcing Petia to ride in the rear where she occasionally whacked the animal in the hind quarters with the end of her hackamore rope.

The trail crested and gave the three a view down onto a stream. A narrow, rickety wooden bridge crossed the ribbon of swiftly running water before the trail wound uphill again.

"Any sound of lurchers?" Giles asked.

Petia shook her head. "Nothing at all today. You don't suppose we've lost them?"

"No, not likely. Just because you can't hear them doesn't mean they aren't back there, sniffing our trail."

"Hadn't we better keep moving?" Keja asked. "This miserable animal is holding us back. Curse you, you long-earred whoreson!" Keja thumped the mule squarely on the top of its head. The mule turned an accusing brown eye around and stubbornly planted its feet, as if daring Keja to continue the abuse.

"Don't worry," Giles said. "I think we can throw them off for a bit by taking to the stream. It seems shallow enough this time of the year. The bridge tells me that in the spring the water must run high."

"How are we going to get down to it?" Petia asked, staring at the steep incline.

"The dogs would pick up on our scent immediately if

we entered straightaway. We ought to take a chance and backtrack a bit.''

Keja shook his head. "I don't like heading back toward our pursuers. That sounds suicidal.''

"Trust me.'' Giles grinned when he saw the sour look crossing Keja's face. No one trusted any of the others— too much. "Petia will hear those lurchers if they get near enough to matter. Since she can't right now, I'm sure we can go back a ways before we leave the trail. When he sees the stream, Segrinn will know we took to the water to hide our tracks. Our best chance is to confuse him for as long as possible, perhaps even duping him into either splitting his force or going in the wrong direction.''

Keja and Petia nodded. It made sense.

"Are we agreed, then? If we lead the animals, it will help. The trail is dusty, and our tracks don't show well. And we can always pray for wind to further confuse the spoor. The dogs track by smell and should get soundly confused right about here.''

It felt good to be on the ground again. They stretched their legs, then tugged the animals around. The mule cooperated for a change. For a quarter hour, they retraced their own tracks. Finally, Giles halted them.

"This looks like a good place for what I have in mind. Find some rags to tie around the animals' feet.''

Keja shook his head in mock horror. "Trust me, he says. Now he wants me to take off what few clothes I have.'' He plucked at the rags he wore. Giles and Petia laughed.

"Poor, abused Keja,'' Petia said insincerely.

In a few minutes, Giles had the hooves of the three animals wrapped. He threw the remaining scraps to the others. "Now do up your own feet. We'll lose them yet. A trick I learned while scouting during the War.''

With their feet bundled as if they headed into the arctic regions, they left the trail. They reached the top of a hill and zigzagged down the other side, finding the rockiest areas. This presented problems for the horses but Keja's mule walked sure-footedly. Giles even thought he detected an air of arrogance and superiority in the beast, as if it said, "What's wrong with you clumsy oafs?"

Silently, Giles pointed toward the stream. He was pleased when they reached its edge, leaving little sign of their passage along the hillside. The hoof coverings prevented the shod animals from leaving revealing nicks and scratches on the rock, and in the few places where dirt graced the hill, only amorphous prints marked their passage. The shallow stream had a gravel bed. Seeing this made Giles actually hope they would elude Segrinn and his lurchers. Giles and his companions would leave no trace at all on such footing.

"Get ready for a long ride," he told the others. "Once we start, we stop for nothing." Giles filled his leather water bag with the fresh water, then led his horse into the stream. He headed upstream; the others followed.

For nearly an hour, the stream remained shallow. Giles's hope that they'd escape Segrinn rose to impossible heights, only to be dashed when they came to a falls in the stream.

"Out," Giles said. He failed to hide from the others his disgust at this sorry turn of events.

"What do we do now?" Keja asked, looking around at the golden hills surrounding them and the deep notch through which the stream tumbled hundreds of feet to a pond below.

"Unless you can turn horses into fish, we climb." Giles pointed up a narrow draw leading into the hills. He didn't have to point out that this might prove to be a box canyon that could cost them precious hours.

"My swimming abilities are minimal," Keja said, then launched off on a spicy, outrageously exaggerated version of his sea trip from Klepht.

Giles let the small thief ramble on until he'd had enough. He cut him off with an abrupt gesture. "If we're going after the key Petia has told us about, we've got to get to the coast and find a ship. Perhaps the one on which you found such fine company."

Keja sputtered and fell silent about his sea-going exploits.

"But the coast is back there." Petia gestured back the way they had come. "How are we going to reach it if we're heading north?"

"The shortest distance between two points is not always a straight line. When you are fleeing, that is." Giles began drawing a map by stacking pebbles from the stream. "There's a major road north of these hills. We can travel west along it, cross through Margaret Pass, and make our way back to Druse Hook. We should be able to catch a ship from there. Anyone got any better ideas?"

Petia sat cross-legged, staring at the ground.

"Petia, you see any problem?" Giles asked.

"What? I'm sorry, Giles. I wasn't paying attention. I've been thinking. I was eager to get away from Segrinn and needed your help. I didn't exactly lie to you about that, but I don't really know where the key is. I mean, it's somewhere near Trois Havres, but I don't know *exactly* where."

"Now you tell us!" Keja exploded. "Here we are on our way to take ship across an odious amount of water, and all you wanted was for us to rescue you."

"You're on the run, too. So you're not out anything."

"Silence, you two," Giles bellowed. "We're not going to get anywhere if we start fighting among ourselves. I don't blame Petia. Segrinn sounds like someone we'd all like to avoid."

"True, but—" started Keja.

Giles cut him off again. "I didn't say I'd search for keys, either, if you'll think back over our conversation."

"Well, are you or aren't you?" Keja asked. "If you're not, we might as well split up this instant."

"I've thought it over. I will. And I don't think it makes any difference whether Petia knows where the key is or not. She knows the general area. We'll just have to keep our ears open and see what happens when we reach Trois Havres. Meanwhile, her arguments about someone tracking you still hold. The men of this merchant l'Karm are going to find you sooner or later if you don't leave Bericlere."

"I suppose you're right," Keja said with ill grace. "Are we ready to move?"

Giles knew the argument was over—this time. The old sergeant detected the seeds of other disagreements blooming, but they would be dealt with when they fully blossomed. Later. They headed up the draw and into the hills.

For over a week they rode, north to Margaret Pass, west over the road. Occasionally, Giles would leave them camped in the forest, ride into a town, and purchase supplies to keep them going. Shopkeepers sometimes raised their eyebrows at the quantities he asked for, but his money silenced questions. Giles never volunteered any information.

When they had crossed the mountains and come down into the grasslands, Giles said, "We near Druse Hook. Before we enter the city, we must be in full agreement."

"We go on," said Keja. "The more I think of the Gate, the more I want to see what lies behind it."

"He talks in his sleep about it," Petia chided. "The moans, the cries of thwarted passion! He calls out for blondes and redheads and brunettes, women of all shadings, to do his bidding."

"There might be more on the other side of the Gate," Keja said. Then he brightened. "But if there isn't, I shall be well enough pleased!"

*   *   *

Druse Hook was a small port with a harbor situated inside a sandy hook continually deposited by the fierce action of wind and restless currents. Giles chose an inexpensive back-street inn, but not before the innkeeper assured him that tubs of hot water came with the price of the rooms. Finding a ship across the Everston might be their prime consideration, but having a hot bath first wouldn't set them back any. As Giles said, "Prime and first are not always the same." And clean clothes followed.

Much refreshed, Giles told Petia and Keja, "I'll go to the harbor and see about passage. The best thing you two can do is stay in your rooms. You are both being sought. Your likenesses may have been circulated by l'Karm or Segrinn."

"I have an odd feeling," Petia said, "that Segrinn has caught up with me. I'm going out and check."

"That's not a good idea, Petia. If Segrinn has followed us here—or decided we would eventually come here—you might be seen. He'd have his men out asking questions. You could endanger both Keja and me."

"They won't see me. They'll see only . . . this."

Giles and Keja watched silently as Petia's body became leaner and took on the characteristics of a cat. Giles blinked and rubbed his eyes when he saw Petia drop to all fours and stalk across the floor. Her hands became paws, her eyes narrowed and the iris grew even more vertically elliptical.

As quickly as the change had come, Petia stood in front of them, again normal.

Giles had seen similar legerdemain during the War. A Trans in his company had been able to assume—or make others think he had assumed—the shape of a snake. Such obvious differences between Trans and human still left Giles uneasy.

"Don't do that again," Keja said uneasily. The small thief rubbed a nervous hand across his lips, then tried to hide his feelings.

"It bothers you, this little secret that we Trans have?" Petia asked, taking an impish delight in her display. "I do it using my empathic powers—it is illusion, partly giving what you want to see and partly hypnotic."

"But your body doesn't really change?" asked Keja.

"I do have some slight ability to alter form, thanks to Cassia n'Kaan's long-ago curse. But mostly it's the reading of emotions and . . . it's hard to describe . . . *meshing* with them."

"You're sure you'll be all right?"

"Oh, yes. I've done this often." Petia headed for the door.

Outside the inn door, Giles watched uneasily as Petia once more became catlike and melted away down the street. She flaunted her talents too openly, he thought. Anything unusual would be commented on by those in the coastal city. While Trans visitors were common enough, especially in seaports, Giles still worried.

Petia roamed the darkened streets of Druse Hook, reveling in the freedom of being away from Keja and Giles. While she thought they both smelled nice, Petia rebelled against the enforced nearness. Her nature required a certain distance that had been denied her while they rode the trail.

Now she ran wild, occasionally meeting a real cat and snarling at it, just to keep in practice. She listened intently at every street corner for the barking of the lurchers, and for an hour Petia quartered the upper town, prowling with no success. Distressed at not finding Segrinn, Petia finally stopped prowling and started thinking.

"Segrinn wouldn't stay at a cheap inn," she said to an alley cat perched on a tall fence. The battered animal stared at her, no kinship between them. Petia ignored that she had invaded the alley cat's territory and continued talking aloud. "With his wealth, and especially after being on the road, he would find the best inn in town. And just perhaps my hunch is wrong. Perhaps he's not here at all."

The alley cat yowled. Petia hissed back, but didn't accept the challenge. She rose and followed a side street toward the harbor. Less than two blocks slipped by her when she heard the barking and followed the sound. Petia felt adrenaline rushing through her body as she neared the inn's courtyard. She hesitated, fearful, listening carefully as the dogs gave voice to their frustrations.

"The lurchers," she hissed. There could be no question.

She moved forward on cat-light feet and sat quietly at the foot of the entrance archway. Segrinn and his men had just arrived and were stabling their horses for the night. The dogs, tied to a wooden hitching rack, snapped and bawled.

Petia crept into the courtyard, crossing near the lurchers, just beyond the reach of their leashes. The dogs yelped at her approach and gave tongue.

"Cat bitch," the leader snarled. "Kill cat bitch!"

A window on the second floor opened and someone shouted, "For the gods' sakes, shut them hounds up."

Segrinn and one of his men dashed out of the stable area, brandishing whips. They laid into the dogs, screaming obscenities at them and cutting at their flanks and hindquarters with the leather. Petia went through instinctual motions of cleaning nonexistent whiskers. Her purring message struck through the sound of swearing and whistling whips.

"Master!" cried the lead dog. "Cat bitch! *Aieeee!*"

Segrinn laid into the beast. Petia watched, taking intense pleasure in the animal's pain.

Another of Segrinn's men came out of the stable. He saw her crouched in the corner of the courtyard. Emotions flowed, but Petia failed to control the man's hatred. She confused his mind enough to make him believe she was nothing more than a cat, but he still picked up a stone from the ground and sidearmed it at Petia. The stone hit where she had been and skimmed into the side of a lurcher, setting off another round of frenzied barking and even more frenzied whipping.

"What are you doing, you oaf?" Segrinn shouted.

"The cat, the cat," the man faltered. "That's what upset the dogs."

Segrinn stared around the courtyard. There was no cat in sight.

Petia heard him shouting as she went over the courtyard wall. "Wretch, if you've finished with the horses, get over here and help us settle down these miserable beasts."

Not a bad evening's work, she thought. With a spring to her step that hadn't been present for too long, Petia returned to the inn.

"The *Marilla Le Bow* departs on the morning tide," Giles was telling Keja as Petia slipped into the room. "I've booked passage for the three of us. Ah, you're back, Petia. What news?"

Petia warmed herself before the small fireplace in Giles' room. Giles saw right away that she was pleased with herself.

"You found them?" Keja asked.

"Certainly did. I got even with the lurchers, too. When I left they were being whipped into bloody ribbons."

Giles looked disappointed. "They're just doing what their nature requires, trying to please a master that's none too kind, from what you tell us."

"I expected something else from you, Giles." Petia defiantly held her head high.

Giles sighed. "And I expected common sense from you. No sleeping in soft beds tonight, then."

"Why not?" Keja cried. "The serving wench in the tavern next door eyed me and I thought—"

"You think with your gonads," snapped Petia, taking her ire out on him.

"We leave," Giles said firmly. "There's too much risk staying here now. The lurchers know Petia is near. They'll be restless all night, and Segrinn eventually will listen to them. The best thing we can do is board the ship tonight before Segrinn posts lookouts on the streets.

"Gather your belongings. I've already sold the animals. An ostler will collect them here in the morning."

"Marram," Petia muttered.

"The pony will be all right," Giles said gently. He just hoped they would be, also.

The harbormaster's crew pulled at their oars, and slowly the ship began to move up the inside of the hook toward the entrance to the harbor.

Petia tensed, leaning over the rail. "Listen," she said.

The sound of barking cut through the inshore breeze. Giles motioned Petia to stay where she was. He walked across the ship to the other rail. A heavy-set man rode his horse onto the wharf. He was accompanied by several other men on horseback and a pack of slender hounds. Segrinn.

Giles lurched, then grabbed the rail as the ship caught the first of the incoming waves at the harbor mouth. He couldn't resist. He waved.

The porcine innkeeper's huge belly rubbed the desk, and his jowls wobbled as he greeted them. Generations of evolution had brought the Trans closer to humans, but this man worked at being a pig.

"Welcome to our fair city of Sanjuste. Will you be staying long?"

Keja had tried not to stare at the hundreds of Trans they had seen along the streets leading from the harbor. He had seen Trans before, but never in profusion.

"Couldn't we find a better inn than this one?" he complained, once they were in their room.

Giles' stare was cold. "You paying?"

"Ah, well, there is that little matter, isn't there?" Keja maintained his aloofness. "I've been meaning to ask a favor of you, Giles. I grow so tired of these rags. The ladies ignore me, and I thought that maybe you could advance me a couple of crowns for a suitable collection of clothing—so I won't disgrace you when we are seen together on the streets, of course."

"Keja, they just don't make many like you. Thank the stars! I'm not giving you a bent copper. If you're half as clever with those fingers as you boast, put them to work. If thievery is your trade, then so be it. Until then, I will lend you some of my clothes."

Giles spilled the contents of his pack onto the bed. He threw a shirt and trousers to Keja.

"But they'll hang on me," Keja complained. "I will look the fool!"

"All right, then give them back."

Chagrined, Keja stripped off his beggar's shirt. Giles' shirt fell over his head and hung loose about him. He stepped behind a modesty screen and changed into the borrowed trousers. They would have fallen off him had he not cinched the belt tightly.

Petia stifled a laugh when Keja came out from behind the screen.

"I look like a scarecrow," Keja said.

"Indeed," Giles agreed, "but a clean one." He hesitated at the door. "Try to stay out of trouble, Keja."

Keja listened as Giles' footsteps faded away down the stairs. "Damn him." He threw his rags in anger at the corner of the room. "Where's he off to?"

"Off to learn what he can, just as I am."

Keja watched Petia leave. He heaved a deep breath and told himself, "Let's see if those fingers are as nimble as they were in Klepht." He flexed them. The crowds in Sanjuste would go home this day lighter in the pouch, if Keja Tchurak had anything to say about it.

Petia felt more comfortable than she had in some time. She was home again. Seeing so many Trans along the street made her remember better days. She wandered through the marketplace, smelling the smells, delighting in the colors, the movement, the voices of the vendors haggling with their customers. She saw Keja slipping through the crowd, his light fingers restlessly moving from pouch to pouch, but Petia didn't care to share her company with him.

She wandered to the river and squatted along its bank, watching the women below washing clothes. Fragments of their conversation floated up to her.

"The Lady Sorceress says that she will keep us close to her."

"But the Flame is the thing; the Flame burns forever in the temple. When the Lady Sorceress is not there, the Flame keeps her in our hearts. She will deliver us from all our woes, and the Flame will make us strong and purify us."

"The Lady Sorceress is the Flame. I heard her say that when she was here two weeks ago. She said, 'I am the Flame, and I will burn for all eternity in your hearts. You yearn for your freedom, and I will bring it to you.' "

Petia moved down the bank to the riverside. She removed her boots and dabbled cramped feet in the water. The conversation surprised her. A cult and a new religion had sprung up around the very Flame Sorceress for whom they searched. A new development to tell the others.

Petia listened to the women while they wrung out the

clothes and packed them into reed baskets for the trip home. They were so serious, so involved, so totally immersed in the Flame and its Lady Sorceress. Power, power gathering. She felt it like the increasing tension before a thunderstorm.

Chapter Twelve

Dimly New, the largest of the three coastal towns comprising Trois Havres, teemed with excitement. The three felt it when they rode into town on the mounts acquired in Sanjuste. Giles reined in to let a small parade of cloaked and hooded penitents cross in front. They walked with heads down and feet shuffling, as if the weight of the world rested on their shoulders. But in spite of their gravity, Giles felt the tension as if it were a thing alive, groping with tentacles to pull in all and wrap them with its vitality.

"A curious place, this one," commented Keja. His expression told more than his words. He was disgusted at so many decked out in religious garb. Monks seldom carried money with them, choosing to beg. How could he rob a beggar, much less a begging holy man?

"The religious fervor carries over, even here," said Petia. "We might not have to seek out the Flame Sorceress. She may come to us if we wait."

"They have the appearance of waiting for divine presence," Giles said, looking around. "The rumors in Sanjuste that this is the place to be prove correct, it seems."

"I'm hungry," grumbled Keja. "The ride was long and—"

"And you're always famished or in search of a willing woman," finished Giles. "The ride amounted to little more than an hour, but there's a likely looking spot."

"I agree, I agree," Keja said. The woman lounging outside the tavern caught his eye. If Giles hadn't led him past, Keja would have forgotten his hunger to spend a few minutes flirting with the woman, who seemed only too inclined.

"She'd just take your money and leave you high," said Petia.

"No, no, you're wrong," said Keja. "She had the look of a seeker of wisdom about her. An intellectual wanting company to compare theories."

"A whore seeking a midday tumble," said Giles.

"You might be right, but still—"

The landlord stopped by their table and interrupted Keja. "Have you come to visit the temple?"

"That we have," Petia quickly said, before Keja denied it.

"The town swells with people who have come from far and near to learn about the Confraternity of the Flame."

"Actually, we are here on a matter of commerce," Giles answered. "But we will undoubtedly listen to what is being said. The people at home will be asking us about the Confraternity. We must be able to portray an accurate picture for them."

"Yes, of course. And where is home?" the landlord asked.

Giles saw hopes of money in the landlord's eyes, full rooms at the inn when they reported back to their associates. "Bericlere. We come from the city of Neelarna."

The landlord's enthusiasm changed to disappointment. "So far away. I hope your business is well transacted," he said curtly and moved on.

"So, this new cult goes by the name of the Confraternity of the Flame," Giles said in low tones. "It bears investigating. We must listen carefully to the street talk, listen to the preachings. The Lady Sorceress, as you heard her called back in Sanjuste, Petia, seems to be the same one you told us of."

"We'll soon see," Petia replied. They wolfed down their meal, eager to be on their way.

They had only been on the street for a few minutes when they saw people greeting one another with a sign made by extending the hand, palm forward and fingers up.

Keja watched with amused superiority. "They speak in riddles. This Confraternity is no more than any other mumbo-jumbo religion."

They heard a maddening array of ritualistic slogans and catch phrases. "Beauty is Flame." "Flame will rule the world." "Flame will burn out the ills of the world." "Flame destroys evil."

In a few minutes they had heard enough.

"I don't understand it," Keja said. "Why do they all greet one another with those phrases?"

"It sets them apart, makes them different, part of a community," Giles said. "It's like a secret password that makes them feel special."

"Sounds crazy to me," Keja muttered.

Farther on, they came to a temple set up hastily in a small warehouse. A hand-lettered sign had been tacked above the door proclaiming: THE TEMPLE OF THE CONFRATERNITY OF THE FLAME.

"Doesn't look like much to me," Keja said as they walked past. "Certainly not worth robbing."

Giles said nothing. This crude temple didn't seem to match the number of converts in the street. By the time the trio reached the center of the town, however, they had passed five more temporary temples, and near the town square they found a new temple. It was nearly finished, but scaffolding still surrounded the exterior where the final touches were being completed on the intricate—and expensive—carved stone facade.

"We've misjudged," Petia said. "Obviously the Flame

Sorceress has acquired a great following—and greater wealth.''

"It might be time for us to become proselytes," Giles said. "We need to find out more about her, to see if she has the key we seek."

A Trans woman stepped up to Petia, thrusting a broadside at her. Petia glanced down at it, a drawing of a flame adorning the top of the sheet.

"Come to our evening service," the woman said. "Hear the good news of our redemption. Learn how we can help you better your life. See how you can find immediate happiness."

Petia studied the woman's rapt bovine face. It was intense, believing, dedicated to bringing others to the temple and its faith. Petia had never seen such mindless intensity in another person. It frightened her.

"What time?" she asked.

"Just after sunset. It is said that the Lady of the Flame will be visiting the temple soon, perhaps this evening."

"Thank you. I'll attend," Petia said.

The woman held up her hand in the gesture the others had used. "The Flame be with you. You won't regret it. It will change your life."

"Not likely," Petia said to Giles and Keja, after the woman hurried on and was out of earshot.

"Have faith," said Keja. "They obviously do. Too much of it, for my taste."

Petia bristled, even though she agreed with him. Admitting that to Keja rankled. "You are too quick to condemn. If this Flame gives comfort, what is wrong with that? You can't know the suffering we Trans have gone through."

"Enough," said Giles, breaking up the incipient argument. "Keja may not know, but I do. And we are here for other reasons, ones not fought out during the War.

"Petia, go to the services this evening. They seem

geared toward Trans, and you'd attract less attention than either Keja or I.''

"What do we do till then?" she asked.

"Wander," answered Giles. "Listen. Try to learn what we can. The more we know, the easier it will be to get the key.''

"If this Flame Sorceress even has it," grumbled Keja, more to annoy Petia than anything else. She snorted and went off to stroll around the marketplace alone, savoring the sights and smells of her native foods, lost in the remembrance of her childhood here.

Petia watched outside the temple, wondering if she ought to enter or not. The coolness of the city after sundown appealed to her more than the stuffy interior of a church. Still, Giles had made a good point about her being less conspicuous than either of the two men. The throng around her was composed almost entirely of Trans of every persuasion: cat, dog, pig, a few avian, and even an outlands elk. Petia reluctantly joined the flow when the summons bell rang three times and was swept through tall wooden doors carved with the depiction of a brazier from which flames leaped upward toward a brilliant light emanating from a gate.

Petia didn't have the chance to examine that gate carving more closely, but it looked a great deal like the Gate of Paradise. Her heart began beating faster at the idea of the Flame cult being based on the Gate.

The Flame Sorceress might actually have the key! Petia would show Keja Tchurak that she could deliver!

Inside, Petia chose a seat near the rear so that she might observe and not have to be a part of the service. The temple filled rapidly until people crowded shoulder to shoulder in the aisles along the side walls. A buzz of conversation rose as Trans waited for the service to begin.

Petia studied the sanctuary area. She had little experience with such things, but it certainly was plain. In the center of a common table—altar?—rested an immense brazier, in which a flame burned. On either side stood large bouquets of freshly cut *linn* flowers. To the right of the altar was a plain lectern.

She waited impatiently, watching those about her curiously as they greeted one another, but without hint of any enjoyment. Their faces were set, deadly serious. What sort of religion had such fervor and yet no joy?

A deep chime rang twice, and the people concluded their conversations immediately and settled into their seats, expectant looks on their mesmerized faces. Petia leaned forward to better see the altar. Everyone else sat back, heads bowed.

A dog Trans entered the sanctuary through a side door. He wore a long, flowing, orange robe and carried a censer billowing clouds of smoke. Petia's sensitive nose twitched from the pungent smell of incense. The Trans went to the altar and bowed to the flame. He slowly turned toward the congregation and, holding the censer high, blew clouds of smoke in all directions. The people sighed and raised their heads once again.

A robed human man and a bird Trans woman entered, each carrying a slim book. They bowed to the flame and took their places before the lectern. Without preamble, they began reciting a litany, alternating between the phrases. After each phrase, the people in the assembly chanted back, "Blessed be the Flame."

Many around Petia closed their eyes, and some had a look of ecstasy on their faces. Petia felt a rising contempt for them, one matching Keja's. She did not understand this charade, and it struck her as pointless, even degrading.

She grew increasingly impatient as the litany droned on. Finally, it ended with a prayer to the Flame, almost screamed by the congregation. After the echoes from the prayer faded, the people on the altar departed. The assembly broke into a babble of conversation and the temple began to clear. Petia could not get away quickly enough. She brushed by the woman who had handed her the broadside earlier. "I'm late," she said. "I must meet someone."

"Come again to our wonderful service," the woman called after her.

"It was awful," Petia explained later that evening. "Chanting that went on and on. The only thing that might be useful was one line of the chant, something like 'O seat of wisdom at Belissiam.' Belissiam is north and west of here, and that may be where the Flame Sorceress resides."

"That makes sense," Giles replied. He worked to get his pipe lit. Sucking in the soothing smoke, he went on. "From what I could learn, the cult started here in Dimly New. There is a large forest west of here in the direction of Belissiam."

"Lesser Green," Petia said.

"That's the name," said Giles. "I watched scores of people leaving town in that direction. Some of the people seemed to have business that way, wagoners, woodcutters, and the like. But there were others who walked with nothing but a sack over their backs."

"Good, we'll go into Lesser Green and see what we can find," Keja said. "Never have I encountered a more boring city."

"None of the women will have anything to do with you?"

"Saw none I'd have on a bet," Keja said testily.

"They think you're a clown in a carnival, wearing those silly garments."

Keja reddened at the Trans' insult. "These are the finest to be had. Can I help it if neither Sanjuste nor Dimly New is at the forefront of fashion like Neelarna?" Keja calmed down, knowing Petia needled him and still he responded. "I will be happy in the wilderness once more, not that Dimly New is far removed."

"I think it would be best if I went by myself," Giles said. "Disguised."

"But I don't want to sit around town," Keja pleaded. "I don't have anything to do now that I have decent clothes again."

"There's one thing you do pretty well, Keja. Visit the taverns and keep your ears open." At this, the wiry thief smiled broadly. "You'll likely hear talk about the cult, but it won't be the same talk that you would hear from members of the temple. I might also advise you to spend a little time in weapons practice. We don't know when we are likely to need skills that are probably a bit stale."

The grin on Keja's face left as if a cloud had blotted out the sun. "The right hand gives and the left hand takes away," he said.

Giles rented horses and a wagon and left Dimly New disguised as a woodcutter. The wagon was empty and the horses handled well. He took the road west and soon came to a fork leading to Lesser Green. Here, he paused to simply enjoy the countryside. Giles had too seldom taken time to reflect on the beauty of woods, the singing of birds, the gentle wafting scent of parti-colored flowers. All those took away the blanket of weariness that had again descended upon the man.

"You're too old for this," he told himself. "But the reward!" The idea of entering the Gate of Paradise held him captive. "Only one may enter," he said softly, "and I will be that one." Heartened by this thought and the bright, fine day, he clucked his tongue and got the horses moving once more.

A mile farther, he pulled over to the side of the road to let an oncoming woodcutter's wagon pass.

"A good load you've got there," Giles hailed him.

"Aye. I don't know how much longer we'll be able to

cut in this forest, though." The old gaffer seemed willing to sit and talk, giving his animals a rest.

"Why's that?" Giles asked. The old man took him at face value—a fellow woodcutter.

"Haven't ye noticed the strange goin's on up in High Forest? Down here it's all right. But there's not much we can cut here worth the mention. Plenty of wood still up in the high forest, but there's people up there keepin' me out. Don't know who they are but they're armed—nasty whoresons they are, too. Best get careful-like when you go up there."

"Can they do that?" Giles asked. "That's open forest."

"Don't know as they should, but they are. I'm not about to argue with a sword. They act like they's got the right, and I don't know no better. Turned me right around, they did and chased me off. I got my load lower down. But if they keep us out, we'll have to go over to Nether Forest. I don't like that. It's a longer haul."

"Who'd they say they were? Who owns that land?" Giles' curiosity was completely aroused.

"Didn't say. Just ran me off. Wouldn't take no argument. Like I say, you best be careful."

"Thank you for the warning," Giles said. He reached behind the wagon seat and handed two apples to the old woodcutter. "These will help your journey. Juicy and sweet, they are."

The man accepted them with a nod, and clucked up his horses. Giles moved back onto the track and continued onward.

Three more times he met people coming down through Lesser Green. The information he received from them matched that from the old man. By afternoon, Giles left the lower forest and entered High Forest. Mentally, he prepared himself to meet these sentries. He didn't have long to wait.

"No farther, woodcutter."

Giles pulled the horses to a stop. He put his finger to his forehead in a sloppy salute. "Afternoon, yer honors," he said.

Three men blocked the road. Two were middle-aged, but one was only a shiny-faced youngster. "You can't go any farther. This is now a private estate."

"But I've always cut wood here." Giles pointed up into the forest. "Up there, you see where that rock sticks out? Just below that."

"Well, no more cuttin' allowed," an older man said. "Yer goin' to have to find another place."

Giles shook his head in disbelief. He looked behind him, as if asking for help in setting these men straight. There was no help behind, and he began again. "I don't understand. I cut wood here since I was a child, used to come with my da. Right up there." He pointed again. "I'll walk up there and show you." He began to climb down from his wagon.

One man lifted a staff. "No, you don't. Just stay up there on your seat. There'll be no gettin' down. And no showin' us where you used to cut. No more cuttin' beyond this point. Do you understand?"

Giles stood on the floorboards in front of his seat. "No, I don't understand. My da and me—"

"You told us. Now we're tellin' you. This is private land. You can't come on it anymore. Now go back."

Giles looked up at the men. "But we can't cut down below. The trees need more growth." He thanked the man he had first met for that information. "We'll have to go clear over to the Nether Forest."

"That's your problem, ain't it? Turn your wagon around and go on back down."

"I'll get my fellows, and we'll be back. Can't keep us out," Giles threatened. "What lord owns this land now?"

"Ain't no lord, mister," the youngest spoke up.

"Hold your tongue, boy."

Giles hid his grin by turning and adjusting the sacking on the wooden wagon seat. He sat and began to turn the team and wagon around for the trip back. "You ain't heard the end of this," he said.

Behind him he heard the young voice. "May you keep the Flame."

Certainly these were devotees of the Flame and the headquarters of the Flame Sorceress was somewhere in this vicinity. He'd found out more than enough to justify fetching Keja and Petia from Dimly New.

The Flame Sorceress entered Dimly New as if she were a queen and the town part of her holdings. Two acolytes went before her, shouting, "Make way for the Flame Sorceress. Make a path to the temple." She bowed right and left as people parted for her, and others came running for a glimpse of the important personage.

Petia nudged Keja in the ribs and said, "She goes to the temple. I'll follow."

Keja said, "What do you want to do that for?"

"We need to learn everything we can about her, dolt. She has the key, remember? And it might make the difference between living and dying. Or doesn't that interest you?"

"I suppose you're right. Indeed, I am interested in living. Go ahead, then. I'll visit another tavern, just like Giles ordered."

"Lucky you," Petia snapped.

The beginning of the service was similar to that of the previous evening, the long litany followed by the congregation's interminable response. Just as Petia wondered if her legs would continue to hold her, an orange-robed priest strode out, ringing a small bell. A hush fell.

"All worship the Flame Sorceress!" he called in a clear, resonant voice.

The woman swept into the sanctuary, made a perfunctory bow toward the flame, and ignoring the lectern, came to stand at the center in front of the altar. She wore a carmine robe that fell to the floor. Around the hem, stitched golden flames licked upward. On the back was embroidered the symbol of the gate from which light emanated, the same as that carved on the temple doors. Hanging from a chain around her neck was a golden pendant shaped like a heart from which flames leaped.

The Flame Sorceress stood in splendor, arms held high, palms inward, as if welcoming the glowing warmth and love from the assembly. When she began to speak, it seemed to Petia that she did not raise her voice, but it reached into the farthest corners of the temple with clarity and power and urgency.

"People of the Flame," she addressed them. "Are you people of the Flame?"

"Yes." A mighty roar attested that they were.

A smile of inordinate beauty crossed the woman's face. Petia shivered a bit; the sorceress knew she held her worshipers in absolute thrall.

"You are humble people, good people," the sorceress said in a soft, beguiling voice. "Your ills are not caused by bad crops or poor trading or fish refusing to jump into your nets. No." The hum passing through the crowd told Petia each of the congregation listened and believed. "*They* are responsible for your woes, the starvation, the taxes. *They* rob you of your pitiful gains and call it for your own good. Are you better paying the lords, when your babies whimper and starve?"

Petia forgot about her tired legs and sore feet as she listened to the sorceress exhort her followers to what Petia could only call treason. Couched so beautifully in phrases that only one versed in the law might see behind, the sorceress skillfully suggested that the ills of these common folk could be laid at the feet of the powerful, of the lords, of the wealthy merchants. With the charisma the Flame Sorceress showed this night, it would not be

long before she revealed to them the holy way of
violence and called for open rebellion.

At last, the diatribe masquerading as a sermon ended.
Another brief prayer finished the service. Petia gratefully
joined the flow leaving.

"Wasn't that a wonderful sermon, so beautiful, so
honest?" a sheep Trans walking beside her asked.

"Indeed," Petia answered, hiding the sarcasm she felt.

The man was garbed entirely in black and appeared to
have had too much to drink. He staggered to the bar,
waving a goblet from which wine splashed. "Landlord,
his name's Grimsmate. You're sure you don't know him?
Fought with him in the War, the bastard. Gonna get even
with him."

Keja sat in the corner of The Maltster's Arms. He had
avoided the weaving drunk when he entered. A flagon
was a joy to be savored. Falling down drunk was
something Keja thought disgusting. It was only on
hearing Giles' name that Keja became alert.

The man continued to wave his goblet and defile Giles'
name. Keja watched the man closely; it became clear that
the man wasn't as drunk as he pretended to be. A drunk's
glazed eyes were not there. This man's eyes blazed clear
and shining, with cunning and intelligence in them, not
stupor.

Keja started to go talk with the man in black, only to
find him gone. Keja frowned, finished his ale and left.
He would be at the inn when Giles returned and warn
him of an enemy.

Giles returned horses and wagon to the ostler, happy to
be down from the hard board seat. He started back to the
inn when a voice called out, "Pardon, good sir. Could I
trouble you for directions to the Kardavi Theatre?"

Giles turned and stared at the man, then shook his
head. "Sorry. I am only recently arrived in Dimly New.

You might inquire of the ostler.'' He pointed out the man inside the stable.

''Thank you, good sir.'' The black-clad man smiled at Giles, turned and walked off, ignoring the ostler. Giles thought that strange, but the entire city seemed filled with strangeness.

Giles never heard the mocking laughter. He was too intent on returning to the inn with his information.

Chapter Thirteen

"I'm certain that the headquarters for your Flame Sorceress is in the High Forest. When they turned me back, I got the impression of many guards. I suspect that the entire perimeter is patrolled. We'll have to be careful."

Giles had recounted his day to Petia and Keja. It was an unsuccessful day for a woodcutter, but successful for their search.

"What do you suppose lies behind the sentries?" Keja asked.

Giles packed his pipe and got it going. "I have no idea. It could be a castle, a cabin, a mansion, a fort. We'll have to go easy and keep our eyes open." Giles puffed until his head vanished behind a cloud of blue smoke. "I doubt those men on the forest road are the only obstacle to finding out. It's going to require all three of us."

Keja spoke up. "Giles, you ought to know that a man was asking after you in a tavern this evening. He bore some grudge against you. He pretended to be drunk, but I think that he was not."

"What man?" Giles asked.

Keja described him as best he could.

Giles frowned. "I may have seen him outside the stables. I have no idea who he might be." He sighed, then pushed it from his mind. They had other items to worry over. "It might be wise to leave town quickly and quietly. From what Petia says, the sorceress and her temples are likely to stir up trouble soon. Before a civil war breaks out, we want her key.''

"If it even exists," said Keja.

"It must," Petia said vehemently. "That symbol—the Gate! It must be the Gate!''

"I suppose I can accept that, as a place to start," Keja said, his air of superiority making Petia want to rip out his throat. Keja smiled, infuriating her further.

By afternoon, they had entered the High Forest. Storm clouds had passed during the night and the sun shone down brightly, dappling humuslike underfooting with the shadows of leaves. The trio moved quietly through the sylvan beauty while keeping a sharp lookout for anyone patrolling.

"How much farther were you able to go on the track?" Petia asked.

Giles squinted up through the forest top at the sun. "Hard to say. I'd guess another half hour's walk. We should go more slowly from this point on."

Petia spotted the first sentries where Giles predicted. The trio stopped immediately and crouched. For a quarter hour, they watched. The guards were the same as the day before, two men and a young lad. Boredom worked its stultifying way into their minds, causing them to stretch and yawn loudly from time to time, but never did they move beyond the open forest glade.

Giles pointed back the way they had come. With Keja leading, they retraced their path through the High Forest until they could talk in guarded tones without being overheard.

When Giles finally halted them, Keja asked, "What now?"

"We set up a minimal camp. We may have to scout for a couple of days. We need some place to sleep dry, build a fire, maybe a source of water."

They found a perfect spot on the interstice between
High Forest and Lesser Green. An old fault line with
fallen boulders created a windbreak. Pure, icy cold water
bubbled up from a spring nearby.

"Get a fire going, Petia. Keja and I will scout the
perimeter to determine what fortification the Flame lady
has built. We may be gone for some time."

"Wait! I'm going, too," Petia said.

"No, you're not," said Giles. "Too dangerous."

"I'm no Gentian Coast beauty who must be protected.
Who went slinking into the inn courtyard to tease those
lurchers?"

"That was stupid," Giles said coldly. "We have no
room for stupidity now. You're not coming with us. No
arguments."

Petia smoldered. "Damned humans. Don't you think a
Trans is good enough to go with you? I've done
everything you've done this far."

"I want to find you here when we return. No matter
how long that takes. Do you understand?"

Petia pursed her lips. "Yes, I understand." She turned
away and stomped off toward the spring.

When she returned, the men had slung their bedrolls,
packs and swords against a large boulder. They had left
with only their daggers.

Still angry, Petia dug into her pack and brought out a
small pot and her mug. Soon she had a small fire going
and boiled water for tea.

Petia slouched against a boulder and sipped the steam-
ing brew. Gradually a calmness settled over her. She
would defy Giles' instructions—but unemotionally, utiliz-
ing those skills that Giles did not seem to want to
recognize.

Petia, too, left her sword behind, preferring to rely on
the skills that were hers by nature. Quietly, she rinsed her
mug in the spring, dried it, and put it away. She covered
the small fire, letting the simple chores drain away her

anger. Petia took one last look at the camp, making certain that all was in order. She fingered her dagger hilt, examined the sky for signs of rain, then melted into the forest.

The men they had first seen in the glade had been replaced by a nearly identical team, no more charmed with their task than the others. Petia spied on them for a short time until she became almost as bored as they were.

A flute sounded its musical note—a signal? Petia slipped away, moving quietly along the forest floor, intent on investigating.

Five minutes of careful movement brought her to a different patrol of guards, seated on a log, playing a game with stones on a board drawn in the dirt. Petia wanted to tell the curly-haired one that he had just made a losing move—but he would discover that soon enough.

Petia backtracked cat-soft until she was halfway between the guard stations. She crouched, listening. Not a sound. She moved forward, watching intently. For long minutes she walked, alert for any sound. Although Petia had spent a fair amount of time on the road in the past two years, she still thought of herself as a town dweller. The forest was silent except for an occasional breeze soughing through the tops of trees, rustling the leaves and sending an occasional one tumbling gently to the ground. The eerie silence made Petia nervous.

She hoped more sentries would appear soon. She knew how to deal with that problem better than with the ominous feeling of the forest giants surrounding her, of unseen and slightly heard beasts stalking about, of things rooting in the soil beneath her feet.

Finally, she saw a clearing ahead. Low to the ground, she crept forward, using the tree trunks to shield her from any spying eyes.

A huge ironbeam tree dominated the edge of the clearing, one limb, thick enough to hold her, branching

out from the trunk. Its leafy, steel-gray foliage would
hide her—if she got up unseen.

Petia scrambled up the trunk, grasped the branch, and
with feline balance, ran along it. She was careful to stop
before her weight made the limb bounce and betray her.
Cautiously, she parted the leaves and looked down on the
clearing.

Beneath her were paths trodden in the grass. They ran
through the clearing into the forest. Petia guessed that
these were the routes used by the guards to go to their
stations.

The paths converged in front of an opening in the side
of a forested hill. It was obviously a natural cave, but
from her perch there was no way for Petia to tell its
extent. She estimated that the entrance was fifteen feet
across and nearly ten feet high. Sniffing, Petia detected
smoke. Tiny vents lower on the hill, in a deep depres-
sion, streamed the fumes from fires hidden inside the
mountainside. She saw no activity.

Petia settled down to wait. She concentrated on the
cave's mouth. Before long, she saw two men come out of
the forest and head straight for the cave. Was there to be
no challenge at all?

Petia saw a flickering just inside the entrance. The two
guards walked to the cave opening and stopped. Petia's
eyes widened as she watched two *things* emerge from the
cave. Human in form, they appeared to be made
completely of flame. The men backed away as the flame
creatures came out into the sunshine. As they walked,
dancing fires shimmered about their bodies, masking all
but general shape and making them even more deadly in
appearance.

The Flame Sorceress surrounded herself with magical
beasts, flame beings. The two creatures carried spears of
fire which they crossed in front of the human guards,
blocking their way. One guard approached, obviously

unwilling. Petia strained to overhear and failed, but a sign or password must have been given. The fiery spears lowered. The men passed between the flame beings, who twisted about searching the clearing, although Petia could not see any eyes. Satisfied, they, too, turned and entered the cave.

Petia studied the paths in relation to the cave mouth, considering how to gain entry. The cave was under a solitary hill, a half mile in circumference and nearly seven hundred feet high. From her vantage, it appeared that the clearing completely surrounded the hill.

How to cross that clearing with nothing to hide her? Other groups of men arrived. Was the guard changing or was this the result of other activities? Had they found Giles and Keja?

When the flurry had passed, Petia took her chance. She left the security of the ironbeam tree and, staying inside the verge of the wood, crept to a position near a path. She studied the distance and realized that the hill itself contained some foliage. Minimal, to be sure, but it would afford cover for her approach.

Patting her dagger to see that it was secure, she zigzagged across the clearing, keeping low. She continued on for several yards up the hill to a bush ox parsley. Petia paused to catch her breath. Looking upslope, she was alarmed to see a guard standing several hundred feet above her.

Why had she not seen him from across the way? Too late for self-recrimination. Petia had to be careful to avoid being seen from above or below. She crept along the hillside, and within a few minutes realized that the curtains of smoke rising from the vents had hidden her from the guard above.

Above the cavern entrance, she closed her eyes and concentrated on her cat form, seeking to bring about the most catlike traits possible. Holding her breath, she waited for her eyes to adjust to the darkness. The contrast

between the bright sunshine and the interior of the cave
made her uneasy.

Flickering light came past a large rock protruding in
front of her, and a narrow trail wound to her left around
the rock. The guards must still be ahead.

Her breathing normal again, Petia moved forward,
staying low to the ground and hugging the stony wall.
The path moved forward only a few feet before rounding
the rock and doubling back in the opposite direction. For
the first time, real fear seized Petia.

"Oh, Giles, Keja, what have I done?" Petia realized
they didn't know she was here, that she was truly on her
own.

The light became brighter. Petia hesitated, looked
behind her, then decided. Curiosity overcame any fear.
She crept forward and peered into a small cavern. Several
flame beings stood at ease with their backs to her.
Bizarre little tongues of flame flickered incessantly along
their bodies. Even though the figures were human
shaped, the flames licking their arms, legs and the back
of their heads, the brilliance at their crotches, they were
decidedly unhuman—and not in the way the Trans were
unhuman.

In the cavern, a dozen Trans worked on weapons.
They were sharpening swords, spear heads, dagger blades.
If the Flame Sorceress brought religion to the cities of
Trois Havres, she also brought violence. The cities would
have to deal with that. For Petia, the problem was finding
the third key to the Gate of Paradise.

She had seen enough; she had news for Giles and
Keja.

Silently, Petia turned to head back into the daylight. A
shadow fell across the cave entrance. Someone returned
from duty outside. Petia sucked in her breath and held it.
The shadow remained motionless, the guard waiting to be
challenged by the flame beings. Petia was caught between
the two.

She desperately hunted for a hiding place in the narrow passageway. None on the ground level. She heard the approaching flame beings, and the light grew stronger, as the creatures came from the depths of the cave.

Above her, Petia spotted a ledge well above the level of a man's head. She leaped for it, scrambling up the slippery stone wall. Tiny bits of displaced rock rattled down as the flame beings rounded the corner. Petia crouched, wishing that she could will herself into the size of a kitten.

"What was that?" The voice of the lead flame being was dry and crackled like the kindling of a new fire.

"Bits of rock always falling from above. Pay no attention. Guard waits at entrance," answered the second. They moved on.

Petia cowered back, petrified. She tried to imagine becoming a piece of rock, of vanishing into the wall. In a few moments, a man passed beneath her, sighing with tiredness. The flame beings trailed behind him and rounded the corner.

Petia let out her pent-up breath and leaped down from her rocky hiding place. The cat Trans breathed silently, holding the image of the flame beings and the guards in her mind, clouding their perceptions, toying with their emotions, so that they would ignore her. Feeling their mental confusion, Petia took the chance and left the cave, then dashed across the clearing and into the relative safety of the forest.

Pausing to catch her breath, she fought to keep from trembling. The emotion-tapping took so much out of her. Petia had bragged about it to Keja and Giles, but there had been little opportunity to practice it. It was definitely not something she did while plying her trade as thief—she shook too much to effectively rob while altering emotional states.

But she had found the Flame Sorceress' underground headquarters, and Giles and Keja hadn't! Happily, Petia flitted back into the forest, merging with shadows and traveling on feet softer than leaves falling on moss.

The expedition went well for Giles and Keja. They stayed outside the perimeter of the sorceress' stronghold, fearing magical wards. From time to time, they saw the usual team of sentries. Giles watched the sun and judged directions from it. The stronghold was guarded by twenty-five teams, if Giles had counted correctly, stationed about five minutes' walk apart. Figuring the distance the sentries covered in the forest growth, the old soldier estimated that the perimeter might be five or six miles in circumference. Seventy-five men on guard at any one time. This gave Giles considerable pause. How many in the stronghold, wherever it might be?

The two men made no attempt to breach the perimeter. It would be enough this afternoon to determine the size of the opposition. As the afternoon wore on, Giles was pleased with their findings.

By late afternoon, they came across a broad, cold, clear stream running southeast through the forest. Giles motioned Keja to rest, and pulled a package of dried meat from his pouch, silently sharing it with him.

The sun slanted down warmly through the trees; the stream burbled merrily; incautious squirrels ventured nearby, openly begging. Giles sat with his back to a log and enjoyed the scene before him. Were it not for their quest for the key, he would be content to homestead in this forest. Not a worry in the world. A nearly perfect life.

Why had he been talked into coming across the Everston to find yet another key? Something to do, an adventure? The War had provided more than enough of that. Adventure had burned out so much inside him—and now he had willingly come along on a new quest. A quest that would probably never be realized, Giles decided.

He motioned to Keja to follow the stream for a ways, then doubled around and headed back for camp.

The squirrels chittered angrily at being ignored, puffed out their jowls, then disappeared into the forest.

"You little fool!" Giles raged. "I *told* you to stay in camp."

"You're just angry because I found more than you did!" she shot back. Her cat traits came boiling out, both from being practiced all afternoon and from Giles' response to her scouting the cave and the flame beings within.

Giles simmered.

"Her time does seem better spent than ours," commented Keja. He winked in Petia's direction. She wasn't sure if she appreciated him being on her side in this or not. She wanted to savor her triumph—alone.

"It leads into the hill?" Giles finally asked.

"Easy to enter, if you're careful. Their security is lax," Petia said smugly.

"You were just lucky."

"You're becoming too cautious for your own good—or ours," she said angrily. "If we are to steal the key from the Flame Sorceress, we must be bold."

"We're not even sure she has the key," said Giles.

"And now you steal arguments from Keja. We *have* to believe the key exists. Otherwise, all our effort is for naught."

"The cat lady has a point, Giles," said Keja. All the thief got in way of response from Giles was a sour expression.

The middle of the night seemed the obvious time to make their way into the cave. Petia led two chagrined men between trees they could hardly see. Her night sight sharpened with every step she took. Petia hardly contained her excitement. For the first time, she had shown her true worth to their venture. Petia nearly purred as she remembered the looks on their faces when she described the cave.

Unerringly, she led them to the ironbeam tree overlooking the clearing. For once, Petia was in command. She silently motioned Giles and Keja to stay put while she investigated. In the dark, she crossed the clearing and entered the cave. No guards—human, Trans, or flame.

She signaled to Giles and Keja and led them to the cave. It was nearly pitch-black in the initial passage, but torches illuminated the walls of the cavern ahead.

"The rock dirties my tunic," complained Keja. "Should we continue?" He nervously licked dried lips. Petia took special glee at his uneasiness.

"I've been this way earlier," she said with great satisfaction.

"Perhaps one of us should stand as rear guard," Keja said. "I volunteer."

Across the empty cavern, they saw other passages leading farther under the hill. Petia raised her brows. Which one? Keja wanted none of them. Giles shrugged. One was as good as another.

Petia led them across the small cave. Giles stopped and rummaged through the crates he found, surprised at the number of weapons stacked along the walls.

"She prepares for a war," he whispered. "Our Flame Sorceress grows bolder."

"Quiet," Petia said, not wanting to give up her leadership yet. They entered a passage and crept forward, Petia, then Giles, and Keja in the rear.

A jumble of rock filled the next cavern. While the roof arched high, the floor some distance below was small in proportion and was occupied by scores of working humans. Stalagtites had grown from water dripping down across limestone spears. Boulders littered the entire area and a narrow rock balcony circled the floor. This small ledge saved them. Sounds of marching men echoed down the corridor behind. Petia gestured for the other two to join her on the balcony. They got up just in time to avoid being seen.

"Give more warning," said Keja in a choked voice. "Fear-sweat is going to leave a permanent stain on my fine clothes if you don't." He edged away from them and sank down to hands and knees, looking pale.

They peered down on the working men and women. The women were involved in mixing some sort of ingredients with mortar and pestle. Flame beings brought supplies from another part of the cave system and carried away what the women had finished. The men were burnishing shields, using a paste that made sparks fly from the shining bronze.

Dust from the powders being ground drifted through the air. A draft from a side passage wafted some toward the trio. Try as she might, Petia could not contain the sneeze. The sound blasted like an explosion. All movement within the cavern ceased.

Six flame beings carrying burning swords trotted to the center of the chamber. Without a glance at the humans working on the cavern floor, they flowed directly to the spot under the ledge where the intruders pressed hard into the wall, trying not to be seen. Giles pushed Keja flat, motioning him to hide.

Keja stayed on his belly, unseen. Flame spears poked up at both Giles and Petia.

With a loud shout, Giles pulled his dagger and jumped. Petia cast a sidelong glance at Keja, then followed Giles, hissing and spitting as she went.

It was over quickly. Giles shouted, "It's no use. We can't get close enough to do them any damage."

Petia had already discovered this. Petia cringed as a flame being's arm came close to her face.

"Steady," Giles murmured to Petia. To the flame beings, he said, "We surrender!"

The spears thrust forward and herded the captives into a side corridor before either could speak further.

Hiding on the rock ledge, Keja held his breath. The human workers began to chatter, and he knew that Giles and Petia had been taken away.

His friends' lives depended on him. He had to rescue them. But how? Keja Tchurak had no idea.

Chapter Fourteen

Hemmed in by the fiery guards, Giles and Petia were herded through one passageway after another. At the end of each succeeding passage, they entered a cavern larger than the one before. Finally, they found themselves in a long stone hall. Flame beings stood along either side, casting an eerie, dancing light across the flagstone floor.

At the far end, steps led to a dais. A woman sat on the throne: the Flame Sorceress. The arms and back of the solid black onyx throne were carved into interlocking flames leaping up toward the ceiling.

To the left of the throne burned a fire trapped in a magnificent brass brazier. The bowl sat atop a tripod of carved nepler wood legs. Flames of crimson and green and azure leaped several feet above the hammered rim of the bowl.

The prisoners, still surrounded by the flame guards, were prodded down the middle of the hall and toward the dais.

"Keep your head," Giles warned. "We don't want to needlessly arouse her anger. There may be a way out of this, if we stay calm." Giles wished following his glib advice were as easy as giving it. Inside, his belly knotted tightly, and his throat constricted to choke him. Of all the dangers he had faced, few had seemed to hold death so imminently.

"But she's trying to subvert the people of Trois Havres to start a rebellion!" Petia protested. Clearly indignant

169

about the Flame Sorceress' goals, the Trans had chosen a poor time to make known her objections.

"That's not our problem."

"It may not be yours, but those are my people, both humans and Trans."

A guard gestured at them to be quiet. Petia flinched away from the fiery arm. She stared with unconcealed hatred at the sorceress upon her fine throne.

"I'll be damned if I'll grovel before her," Petia muttered.

"We've no choice," Giles whispered, as he bent to kneel. "Better to live and fight than to die needlessly."

Petia resisted only until the flame being by her side reached his burning hand toward her back to push her down. She ducked out of the way and crouched on the floor. The flame being reached again and Petia knelt, seething.

"You cannot resist my flambeaux." The voice rang out, calm and silky and beguiling.

Petia and Giles looked upward to the throne. The Flame Sorceress lounged indolently, one slender, well-turned leg crossed over the other. Her flame-colored silk gown set off auburn hair that cascaded down her back and framed her white oval face in soft waves. Giles had to admit she was an overpoweringly beautiful woman. Her splendid proportions held only one flaw—her lips pulled into a thin and cruel smile.

"None sneaks into my stronghold," the sorceress scolded. "People wishing to join the ranks of my beloved followers do so at one of my many temples. They do not come under cover of darkness, creeping like sneak thieves. Nor do they disguise themselves as woodcutters." She looked at Giles. "That surprises you, does it not?"

Giles hid his inner turmoil well. The men who had challenged him had not seemed bright enough that they would report back so accurately. What else did this lovely, dangerous woman know?

"And our angry young Trans here, part cat, from the eyes. Useful blood, is it not, my dear thief? What did you think to find here? Wealth?"

Petia glared up at her. "We wondered about this new cult. You've gathered quite a number about you, haven't you? Followers mean power. Power corrupts so easily, doesn't it?" The softness of Petia's voice nearly matched that of the sorceress. Giles tried to silence her but the Trans rushed on. "Temples where the people nearly swoon with the faith that you've preached to them. You would pervert that faith to lead them in rebellion against their lords. Who would wield the power after a civil war? Why, a natural leader, such as yourself. Is it not so?"

"You do not believe in my teachings? I offer these people a better life than any they will ever have on this world. A life with a glorious hereafter."

"Oh, yes," Petia said bitterly. "A life which can neither be proved nor disproved. In the meanwhile, it is a fertile field that you plow. Hundreds—thousands—of people manipulated, made to spread dissent, sapped of their coin so that you may finance your rebellion. People that can even be molded into an army when the time is ripe."

The sorceress uncrossed her legs and sat forward, no longer the image of calm. "I do not need those people. I have unlimited power of my own." She took a deep breath and composed herself. "Enough." The sorceress rose from her throne. "You doubt my powers. You lie to me. You care not a whit for the people of this country. I do.

"What you really came for is a key—supposed to open a gate to Paradise like the one gracing my temple doors. You'll never find that key, and you'll never get to Paradise. My followers will find Paradise here in my teachings, in their own land, before you find yours."

Sparks showered from the end of her fingertips, then burst into lambent flame. The fire grew. The sorceress flexed her fingers and drew the image of a human in silvery, shimmering air. Another eye-searing flame materialized before her, still amorphous but rapidly taking form. She gestured grandly, and he flowed away with sinuous grace to stand beside her throne.

"You think me a fool. I see it in your eyes!" She held her hands together, as if molding clay. With the suddenness of lightning in the twilight, she flung a fire ball over their heads. Giles and Petia turned in time to see it hit the floor, scattering flame in all directions. Gradually, as if it held a life of its own, the flame flowed into a pool.

From the pool arose a monstrous form, towering nine feet tall, with a torso as massive as a tree trunk. Long arms hung from broad shoulders, arms so powerful that they could easily crush a human.

"None stands against the life I create."

The creature stood, swaying from side to side, not knowing what it was supposed to do. The Flame Sorceress gestured, and the monster melted back into the pool of flame and slowly died away. She flung another ball that turned into a six-foot-long lizardlike beast with a flickering tongue of flame. A third blossomed into a small tree with branches that waved, seeking for prey to burn. A fourth became a snorting, pawing beast with horns blazing so brightly Giles averted his eyes. It bleated plaintively at the sorceress, waiting for her command to charge, to bring the destruction for which it had been created.

"You seek a paltry key while I offer salvation!" A flick of her hand dismissed the fire monsters. She stretched out both hands, and from her fingertips flew lances of lightning that struck the wall near the entrance to the hall. Spears of searing brilliance followed. Next came balls of fire that stuck to whatever they hit, as if they were burning pitch.

The awesome power truly frightened Giles. Neither Giles nor Petia could deny that the sorceress commanded vast magical power. What scared Giles was the way she became more intense with each demonstration. She was caught up in her own power and the pleasure of flaunting it. Her ambition—and viciousness—knew no bounds.

"There, unbelievers! You came seeking a key. Don't deny it. I know. You will never find that key to Paradise. You do not need that key. All you need is to follow me. It is within my grasp to give you all the Paradise you need.

"The key is nothing. A piece of gold said to open the gates. And what will you find behind the gates? No one knows. Hundreds of years have passed since the key was forged. It was nothing more than a symbol of a welding of tribes, primitive peoples with primitive ideas. Do you believe that you will find riches? Ha!"

The Flame Sorceress paced back and forth in front of her throne, breasts heaving in passion, brown eyes blazing, her voice rising. "Here, here are riches, power. You say I manipulate the people. Yes, I admit it. I manipulate the people to bring them their own wealth and happiness. Their paradise is here in their own land. I will show it to them, I will lead them. They adore me. Together we will bring the throne out of this underground hall, and place it in Dimly New. We will become a proudly united people, human and Trans. Wealth and power will flow to me because of my leadership. Nothing can deny me, nothing can get in my way, not you or the pitiful leaders of the coastal cities."

"She's raving," Giles whispered. "She's going to kill us, no matter what we say."

"Then let's try to escape!" Petia hissed angrily.

"There's still Keja. Wait. Play for time."

The sorceress' loud ravings fell to abrupt silence. The change proved as chilling as her insane rage. When the Flame Sorceress spoke again, it was with a quietness that was in nerve-jangling contrast to what had gone before. Delivered in a sibilant, even voice, it sent shivers through Giles' soul.

"Meddlers." She pointed at Giles and Petia; they both flinched, waiting for the leaping flame sent to devour them. "A small pile of charred ashes, is that what you bargained for when you sought to rob the Flame Sorceress? You think me mad. I see it in your eyes.

"No, no burning here. I grant you a brief reprieve. When I have liberated the people of Trois Havres, there will be a celebration. The lords and merchants will be driven forth from their castles and mansions. A pyre is what will satisfy the people. A pyre on which to burn the oppressors. And you two shall join the lords of power and commerce on the pyre.

"No key, Grimsmate and Petia. Only death in purifying flame."

She gestured to the flame beings. "Take them away. Be sure that the cell bars are close enough that our little cat cannot slip between them."

The Flame Sorceress sat down heavily, one slender leg draping over the other in what might have been a seductive display had not her clouded face shown only darkness and death. Giles and Petia marched the length of the hall and out of the door, their flame guards close enough to make their skin prickle.

"She didn't kill us outright," said Petia. "For only ten seconds alone with her!" Claws sprang forth; the flame beings moved nearer, their body heat effectively preventing an escape.

"Just because she didn't kill us doesn't mean it's still not within her power," said Giles. He wondered how acute the senses of the flame beings were. All he might say to Petia would be reported to their mistress, he decided. "Say nothing more."

Petia nodded glumly.

They moved through one passage after another, cross-

ing smaller caves between. Finally, a flambeau motioned
them into a small nook several feet above the floor.

Another of the flambeaux stooped to the floor. With a
flourish, he formed a bar of intense flame running from
floor to ceiling. He repeated the motion every few inches
from one side of the nook's entrance to the other.

The flame creatures turned without a glance and
marched away. Giles and Petia were imprisoned behind
bars of flame.

"What will we do, Giles?"

Giles put his hand on Petia's arm. "The first thing is
get a bit of sleep," he said, giving her soldier's advice.
"We'll think better when we've rested."

"But we've got to get out of here!" Petia was near to
panic.

"We will, we will." Giles took her hands, forcing
Petia to look into his eyes. "Stay calm. We're warm,
we're dry. Maybe we'll even be fed. We won't be killed
for a while. And Keja is somewhere near. They obviously did not find him. For all her seeming omniscience,
the Flame Sorceress missed Keja."

"You think that Keja can help?" Petia asked. "I'm
not sure he's much good for anything."

"He is abler than he shows. Underneath the peacock
posturing and womanizing lies a brave soul."

Petia grimaced. "All right. I'll try to be calm." She
flinched away from the flaming bars again. "I hate fire,"
she said, almost too low for the man to hear.

"At least we'll be warm," Giles said. "We could be
sleeping outside in the cold."

"Damn you, Giles Grimsmate." Petia hissed, then
curled into a tight ball.

Keja Tchurak entered the cavern, swinging stride
confident. He wanted it to appear that he belonged. The
people looked up from their work and automatically gave

the ritual sign. Keja returned it, hoping that it was
correct.

"Who are you? Where are you going?" one of them
asked. Keja's heart clogged his throat; the sign had been
wrong. The cult had put out his description. Something
so small that he had missed it gave him away.

His thief's nerves took over. No great outcry had risen.
This was only an innocent query, not an accusation.

"I'm fresh in from Dimly New," Keja replied without
so much as a quaver in his voice. "I've been sent to
question the prisoners. Where were they taken?"

"Probably to the cells." The man who answered
gestured to the left with his head.

Three passageways led off from that side of the cave.

"I've gotten turned around." Keja laughed at his own
supposed stupidity. "These caves and passages can
confuse me so easily. Which leads to the cells?"

Two women giggled at Keja's seeming embarrassment.
He graced them with a boyish smile and a deep bow.
Toward a comely one, Keja even ventured a quick wink.
The man said, more brusquely now, wanting Keja away
from the women, "The middle one."

"Thank you," Keja said. He made the ritual sign
again, and for good measure added, "The Flame keep
you." He disappeared into the center opening with
relief—and some regret. The one woman, girl actually,
had been quite pretty and more than a little smitten by his
charms. Keja sighed. Giles and Petia needed rescuing.
Then he could seek out the lovely girl and assay the
limits of her infatuation with him.

He was actually beginning to enjoy this.

As he neared the other end of the passage, Keja saw
light flickering on the floor of the next cave. He entered
cautiously. Bars of liquid flame closed off the cell.

He crept silently across the floor. The bars were so
closely spaced that he couldn't see any prisoners within.

Squinting, he made out dim figures. He put out his hand and nearly burned himself on the bars.

"Giles, is that you?"

Giles stirred in his sleep. Petia was leaning against his shoulder asleep. She seemed to be purring.

"Giles," Keja whispered, louder this time.

"Hmmph?" Giles opened his eyes cautiously. "What?"

"It's me. Keja."

Giles came awake and put his hand over Petia's mouth. She snorted and nearly bit him as she, too, awakened.

"How'd you get here?"

"How do you suppose? Master thief and sneakiest of sneaks," Keja bragged. "How do I open the bars? This is unlike any prison cell I've ever seen, not that I've been incarcerated overmuch."

"Let me think." Giles shook the fog from his head. "Remember the passageway at the back of the hill that we found yesterday?"

Keja nodded.

"There was a stream nearby where we rested and ate. If you divert that stream into the cave system, we could drown the flame beings—her flambeaux, the sorceress calls them."

"Sounds like a good plan," Keja said sarcastically.

"Flood the cave," Giles ordered. "I have a hunch that the sorceress derives part of her power from the flame that she keeps around her. Torches burning all over the place, a brazier by her throne. She's mad, absolutely insane."

"How am I supposed to divert the stream?" Keja asked.

"Dig a ditch into one of those passages, then dam up the stream. Cut some logs, brush, rocks, anything to divert the stream into that passageway. They must all connect and run into the main cavern."

"What about you?"

"When the water runs in, it will seek the lowest level.

We're not far above that. The water will put out these flaming bars when it reaches here. There should be a fair amount of panic. We'll find our way out.''

"But what about the key? Do we even know it's in here?" Keja asked.

"I'd bet my last coin on it, from the way she talked about it. We don't know where, but we'll figure that out after we sweep all these flame things out of the cave. That's first. Go now, or you'll be in here with us."

"You're right," Keja said. "It looks warm and comfy in there, though. You all right, Petia?"

"I hate fire," Petia said. "But we'll be all right. Just do as Giles has suggested. I can't get out of here fast enough."

Keja started to reach through the bars to touch them, give them encouragement, then thought better of it. The cuff of his jacket started to char. Instead, he raised his hand and gave them the ritual Flame sign. "Don't go anywhere," he chuckled. "May the Flame keep you."

"When I get out of here," Petia promised, "you'll pay for that remark."

"One more thing, Keja," Giles said. "Watch out for any line of flame that seems to run across the floor. It might burst into some monster creature."

"Why don't I bring some dirt and put it on these bars?"

"Do you see any dirt in the caves? It's all rock. You'd have to go outside and come back again. We can't risk it. Divert the stream. We'll worry about the rest of it."

Keja did wave this time. Cautiously, he made his way out of the cave. Giles watched the wiry thief vanish, hoping his trust in the man wasn't misplaced. The bars of the cell seemed to get hotter by the minute.

Chapter Fifteen

Keja paused to wipe away the sweat rolling from his forehead and into his eyes. He didn't remember working this hard in his entire life.

"I know now why I decided the life of a thief was for me," he complained, his muscles aching abysmally. Manual labor was something he had always tried to avoid.

Boots soaked and feet cold, he cursed the broad stream running down swiftly from the mountains. When he and Giles had camped the day before, they'd thought it rose up from underground; it merely ducked under the surface for a short way. Keja saw no other way for the water to be so crystalline clear and as cold as ice. Twice, Keja stumbled on slippery rocks to catch himself on his hands, but not before the front of his precious tunic was soaked.

" 'Tis not enough Giles and Petia get themselves into a cage of fire. They demand I ruin my clothing to rescue them. Pah!" This was not all he ruined. Keja examined his sword and dagger. Their edges were nicked and dirty and would require extensive retempering to be usable again. If this crack-brained plan worked, Giles would owe him new weapons. And a new tunic and jacket. And even a chance to rest in Dimly New. The one woman in the market *had* looked upon him with some real interest.

He stood, rubbing his aching shoulder and viewing what he had accomplished to this point. The stream still rushed by downstream, but his hard work had piled boulders along the shore and a ditch ran in a straight line from the smoke vents in the rocky hill to a spot just short of the stream. It would take Keja only a few minutes to open the intervening space and send the burbling stream directly down into the cave through the vents.

Then the fight would begin in earnest. Keja didn't fool himself that the human guards would allow the flood to pour into their cave without blood being spilled.

His rest over, Keja reached for the sword again. His body ached and his joints froze. "I know what Giles complains about now," he muttered. Keja never wanted arthritis to seize up his bones permanently. Better to die in some noble venture.

The small thief seized a boulder and wrestled it into position along the stream's bottom. Standing knee deep in the water, he placed the stones with all the care of an uplands beaver. Side by side, he nestled stones of all sizes, then dabbed in mud. When he reached the opposite side of the stream, he was pleased with the first layer of foundation. Keja struggled on, placing another row parallel with the first.

He placed a third row on top of and between the two foundation layers. Some of the rocks now stuck out above the surface of the water. The water flowed between the rocks, seeking a way through, trying to continue its way downstream.

Keja noticed that the water now rose to his thighs. He looked along the bank and saw that the water was rising nicely behind his makeshift dam. He tested the stones for solidity, then began laying cut ironbeam branches along the upstream side, blocking the dam more effectively. He was so pleased with his engineering feat that he no longer cared that he was shivering cold and wet nearly to his waist.

For another hour he labored, pausing only occasionally to attempt to relieve the pain in his lower back. When he had finished, Keja panted in exhaustion. But he felt that the ditch was adequate to channel most of the water into the cave system.

"Better than any dozen men might have done," he said with some pride. "Even if they did know what they were doing, this is better." Here and there rocks tumbled from his dam and let tiny rivulets through. The lifetime of the dam had to be measured in hours—or even minutes.

"No reason to wait," he said, wiping his hands on his trousers. Keja winced at the sight; streaks left by his dirty fingers turned the once fine trousers into a stripped mess. Ignoring the filth and damage done to his clothing, Keja tore into the few remaining feet between the ditch and the stream. Churning, eager water helped him eat away the dirt as it found its way into the virgin path. The pressure behind the dam now had a new outlet and took it with a startlingly loud rush.

Keja leaped for the bank. It collapsed under his feet, and he went down with a windmilling of arms and legs. For one last time, the cold clear water won. Helplessly flailing, Keja was swept along by the powerful force. Even as he foundered, sputtering, he laughed out loud at his success. He eventually found his feet and staggered out of the ditch, dripping mud and water and laughing insanely. He had done what Giles had asked. The water poured forth and blasted its way down into the cavern through the smoke vents.

All he had to do now was stop the guards trying to redivert the stream. Keja hefted his nicked and battered sword and sloshed forward.

"What if Keja succeeds? What will I do?"

Giles looked at Petia. She trembled, and clutched herself as if freezing.

"What do you mean? You'll follow me, and we'll get out of here, one way or the other."

"Giles, the fire bars are bad enough. I hate them. Water is even worse."

"Listen, young lady," Giles said sternly. "You've done splendidly up to this point. Whatever happens, you'll do fine. I have a great deal of faith in your reserves. I may not trust you with the keys, but I have no doubts about your abilities. Keja's, either." Giles warmed inside. It had been a long while since he'd had to give such a speech. He remembered the new recruits, just before going into battle. All had required some small encouragement—it varied from soldier to soldier.

Some needed to believe they were invincible, that nothing could harm them. They usually fought with reckless abandon and survived. The ones, like Petia, who doubted their own abilities, even for an instant, died. Giles tried not to become attached to those under his command in the War. Too often, he had, and it gnawed at his guts when they died.

Petia's dying would end this crazy quest for the key, whether he lived or not.

A flambeau entered the cavern from a passageway across from their prison. A woman carrying a bowl followed three paces behind it. From the haunted expression on her face, she feared the flame being.

The flambeau stooped before the burning bars. It placed its hand at the juncture of floor and bar. The flaming bar shimmered and went out like a candle flame in a high wind. The creature did it again to the next bar, then stood back and motioned impatiently to the woman.

She hurried forward, stepping cautiously past the flaming form and pushed the bowl through the empty space between the bars.

"Food," she said, and backed away fearfully.

With two quick gestures, the flambeau set the bars back in place. He turned and marched away, leaving the woman to find her own way back to whatever section of the caves she had come from. The woman cast a fleeting glance at the two prisoners, then disappeared.

"It looks as if we eat," Giles said, sniffing the odors coming from the covered bowl. "The sorceress doesn't want us starving to death, at least."

"Do you really believe she intends to burn us on a pyre?"

"She meant it when she said it." Giles moved the bowls to a spot between them on the ledge. "Her madness reminds me of a lieutenant I served under during the War. He never understood why the enemy refused to fall into his little traps."

"What happened to him?"

Giles looked sadly at Petia. "He died."

Petia paled. "You mean his own troops killed him? That's awful!"

"The captain replacing him gave a commendation to the one who drove the dagger into the lieutenant's kidney." Giles chuckled. "I still have the medal, somewhere." Petia just stared at him. Giles sobered and said, "Given another rage like the one we witnessed, the Flame Sorceress could order us burned and with no remorse."

Petia shuddered.

"Don't worry about it. Let's see what we have to eat. We'll need strength if—when—Keja is successful."

The stew did not look appetizing, but they both ate hungrily. Petia ignored the grease floating on top and dug in. There was little meat, but potatoes, carrots, and turnips made it wholesome enough, even if she did prefer rare steak to vegetables.

"A loaf of bread would have rounded it out," Giles said, "but complaining to the management will do us little good."

He set the bowl down, and took out his pipe. When he had it nicely packed, he looked around the floor for a twig or a sliver of wood. Finding none, he looked at the flaming bars. "All this fire, and I don't think I can light this damned smokepot."

"Couldn't you hold your head sideways and—"

They were interrupted by shouts echoing through the tunnels.

"I wonder what that is. You don't suppose . . . Keja?"

The shouting became louder. Footsteps resounded from the walls. People were running in all directions, panicky. Voices died away and then came closer again. Neither Petia nor Giles could tell whether the shouting was near or far away.

Like cannonade, one word came through clearly.

Water!

"He's done it! Keja's diverted the stream into the cave. I'm sure of it." Giles swung around, getting feet under him, ready for instant response.

"What do we do now?" Petia asked.

"Wait. We can't get through these flaming bars. We have to wait until the water reaches the bottom of the bars and extinguishes them."

Petia shuddered and sucked in her breath. "I hate water as much as I do fire."

"We'll make it," Giles said.

They sat, listening to the shouts continuing to reverberate through the caves.

"Look." Giles pointed to a passageway across from their prison. Water was seeping slowly from the entrance and spreading across the cavern floor. "I think that this is the lowest level of the caves. I don't know if there's enough water there to do us any good. It's coming in too slowly. It's got to rise faster than that." Giles rocked forward to grip the bars and shake them. Only Petia's restraining hand kept him from nasty burns.

They heard feet sloshing through a tunnel somewhere. Nearby?

Filthy and mud-splashed, Keja staggered out of a

passageway. "Thanks be to Dismatis and the other poxy gods. I didn't think I'd make it."

Keja collapsed outside the burning bars. "I've run most of the way. Except when I was staggering and falling. I don't know if this is doing any good or not, Giles. It's not filling the caves fast enough."

"Never mind that. Get us out of here. Throw water at the base of these bars."

Keja crawled over to a small pool of water puddled in a cavity in the floor. He cupped his hands and tried to crawl back on his knees. The water dribbled through his hands.

"Keja! Stand up and do it properly," Petia cried, almost mad with anguish.

"So say you, lady. You haven't just run a couple of miles." He propped himself up and struggled to his feet. Carefully this time, he cupped his hands and staggered back to the bars. He lowered his fingers and let the water run out onto the base of one bar. The flame sputtered but did not go out.

"Needs more water," Petia coaxed. "Here, use this." She threw him the empty bowl through the flames.

Keja staggered to the pool, filled the bowl with water and came back. The water poured out in a tiny stream. The flame sputtered and winked out.

"One more bar, Keja, and we're free."

After several more trips and what seemed a hundred gallons of water, a second bar was extinguished. Giles guided Petia between the remaining flaming bars, then stepped after her.

"You've got to go back, Keja. I hate to ask it of you. You've done a marvelous job so far, but it's not enough."

Keja looked at Giles, despair in his eyes. After a moment, he nodded and said grimly, "Yes, I know you're right. If it's going to do any good, there has to be more water. I don't know what happened. I was sure I had the entire stream blocked off. Probably didn't do it well enough—or I didn't kill enough guards trying to undo all my handiwork.'' Seven human guards lay dead from Keja's battered blade. ''What are you two going to do?''

''Go look for the key,'' Petia said. ''It's here, and my guess is that it's in the throne room.''

''Where?'' Keja asked.

Giles described where they had been taken when they were captured. ''When you've finished diverting all the stream, come back here. Try to find us. We'll be looking for you—and we'll probably need your help.''

''Good luck in finding the key. I'd hate to have ruined a perfectly good suit of clothes only to find the key didn't exist.'' Keja stumbled once crossing the cavern, then his spirits seemed to lift. His body straightened. He hurried into a passageway and was gone.

''Which way?'' Giles asked. ''Do you remember?''

''I think so,'' Petia said. She pointed down a passage. ''Follow me.''

Water bubbled up everywhere. But Giles had been right in his assessment of its volume. Petia and Giles waded through it up to their ankles. At the moment, however, it was flowing downward, seeking the lowest levels of the cavern system.

''At his rate, it will take forever to fill this damned place,'' Giles muttered.

Petia looked back at him. ''Let's not worry about it. It caused a furor and got us out of our cage and people are too busy to notice us. I hope Keja got out.''

''So do I,'' Giles agreed. ''If he can divert more water, there's a good chance to flood this place right out of existence.''

''We've got to find the key before we do that.'' Petia pressed on. She had a good memory for the route along which they had been herded, and she unerringly found the right turnings.

"Look." Petia pointed. Ahead of them a flambeau came out of a passageway. Seeing the water streaming across the floor, it turned and fled.

"They won't be in our way," she said.

"The only problem is that they'll seek the higher caverns where it's dry. That means they'll be gathered around the sorceress."

To their right, another flambeau appeared at the tunnel entrance. It looked at the cavern floor, awash with water, and began to retreat. From behind it, water rushed down the passage. The water hit its feet, and the flame being literally flickered out of existence. Feet, ankles. As each limb was extinguished, the being sank lower to the floor. Knees, waist. The torso steamed and hissed as water splashed upward. Its mouth opened in a crackling scream as the water washed over its head. Then it was . . . gone.

Giles and Petia looked at each other. Their emotions were in tumult. On the one hand, the enemy was dead and legions more would surely follow. Yet, watching even a flame creature meet its inexorable demise in such a fashion was horrible. Giles shuddered as the image of a butcher disjointing a beef flashed through his mind.

"On, go on." He gave Petia a shove to cover his thoughts. There was no need to express them.

Petia hurried through a passage and into the next cavern. Humans and Trans were gathering goods helter-skelter and streaming in the direction Giles remembered as the entrance to the cave system. They paid little heed to the pair.

"Up there." Giles grabbed Petia's arm and spun her around. "That way to the hall."

A scream ripped through the cavern and echoed around the dripping gray limestone walls. They heard the Flame Sorceress taking out her frustrations on any unfortunate enough to be within her sight.

"Idiots, cretins. We'll all drown! Do something!"

Giles and Petia drew near to the cavern containing the

throne and watched. The Flame Sorceress paced back and
forth, gesturing wildly at the flambeaux surrounding her.
She shouted orders at her flaming soldiers; no human
guards were in sight.

"Where is the human captain of the guard?" she
screamed. "Get him here at once. We must move the
gold."

The madwoman had not yet realized that her flambeaux
would be extinguished the instant water flowed into this
cavern.

Giles murmured, "Hurry, Keja." The old warrior
stepped out into the cave.

"There are no humans, sorceress," he yelled. "They
are deserting your caverns, trying to save themselves
from drowning."

The sorceress stopped at the sound of Giles' voice.
"You!" she screamed. "You and that cat woman.
You're responsible for this."

She flung out her hand and a sparare flashed from the
end of her fingertips. The flaming arrow hurtled across
the cavern, striking Giles in the left shoulder and piercing
the flesh just below his clavicle. It hung there, burning.

Petia leaped to his side. She grabbed the burning shaft
and pulled, wincing as it burned her hand. She flung the
arrow away. It was consumed before it hit the floor.

Giles clapped his hand to the wound. A small flame
still burned where the sparare had entered, searing the
open wound. Immense pain clouded his senses with a red
veil of agony, and he slumped to the floor.

The Flame Sorceress seemed to dismiss the pair. She
did not even deign to acknowledge Petia. She turned to
her soldiers and once again began screaming contradic-
tory orders.

Petia lifted Giles by his good arm and dragged him
into the nearest passageway. He slumped once again,
sitting in the muddy water running around him. His face
mirrored the pain wracking his body.

Petia tore the cloth of Giles' tunic away from the wound. The sparare had gone deep, making a red and ugly wound. With impossible speed, the wound already festered. The complications this would cause if she did not do something spelled Giles' death. She reached beneath her tunic and tore a piece from her white under-tunic.

She made a compress and held it against the wound. There was no way to keep it in place. "Can you hold it there?" she asked.

Giles nodded, his eyes squeezed shut. He put his right hand to the cloth and weakly clutched it. He realized that he must stop the bleeding. But the mounting pain approached the unbearable.

Giles sat, head bowed, grimacing from time to time. Petia stood over him, watching him suffer, patiently waiting for him to determine that he had the strength to go on. Water continued to flow around them. It was well over Petia's ankles now, and flowed over Giles' thighs.

"Giles. Giles!" Petia had to repeat it. "We've got to move. There's more water. Can you get up?"

Giles looked up at her, pain dulling his gray eyes. His left arm hung loose, but he pushed his right hand against the floor and managed to get over on his knees. Petia helped him to stand, but she realized that it took a great effort on Giles' part. The sparare carried not only the burning but magicks intended to give a slow death.

"I'm sorry," he said. "Been wounded worse than this, never felt so weak. Sorry."

"Let's get out of here." Petia took his good arm.

Giles shook off her hand. A look of determination came over his face. "No, we've gotten this far. We search for the key," he muttered. "There's no better time. Confusion everywhere. Where's the audience hall?"

"Dammit, you can hardly stand. Let me help."

With Giles staggering by her side, Petia crossed the

cavern. They came out of the passageway facing the
entrance to the sorceress' grand hall. Giles seemed to
gain strength when he sighted the black onyx throne.

He removed Petia's helping hand and said, "I'll be all
right. Let's search that hall."

The water was rising faster now. It washed around
their calves as they entered the hall. The dais still stood
above water but not for long. They forced themselves
through the water, each step an effort. Behind them they
felt a surge of water. The level began to rise rapidly.

"Keja did it," Giles said, and he smiled for the first
time since the sparare had injured him.

They had gone only a few steps farther when they saw
the brazier toppled by a cresting wave. The flame went
out with a loud sizzling audible throughout the cavern.
The tide ebbed, then surged once more as the pressure
behind it mounted. The throne was picked up and floated
off the dais, as if it were little more than a child's toy
boat.

"Giles, we can't find anything now. It's getting
dangerous. We've got to get out. If we stay here, we'll
drown."

"So close." Tears came to his eyes. From pain? Or
frustration at being so close, so damned close? "But
you're right."

Together they waded from the hall, feeling their way
with their feet. They no longer saw the cavern floor
beneath the water. One of them would surely have fallen
without the other's support.

As they left the Flame Sorceress' audience hall, they
saw the water littered with objects floating through the
caverns. Wooden cases. Tables and chairs. Bodies face
down. Even small stone implements caught in the
maelstrom.

Giles held the cloth to his wound again, depending on
Petia to take the lead and find the way out of the aqueous
nightmare the caves had become.

"Damned key," he muttered. "Who started this? Where's Keja?"

"Let's hope he didn't make it back," Petia said in a choked voice.

Giles staggered, light-headed, when he saw the wall of water rushing across the cavern toward them. Trapped— and unless they could hold their breaths for hours, dead.

Chapter Sixteen

"How do we get out of here?" Giles yelled. The water swirled around their knees and the massive tidal wave blasting toward them spelled certain doom. People struggled through the water from passage to cavern to passage, seeking to save their own lives. Flotsam floated on the water, bobbing and tossing higher and higher, with some of the bigger pieces jamming into exits and creating barriers.

And the wall of water rose, seemed to pause, then rumbled like a thunderstorm as it washed away all life before it.

Petia pointed, the roar too loud to shout over. Giles never hesitated; to do so meant instant death. They flung themselves into the side passage. Giles felt a giant, watery hand grip at his body, squeeze with cruel intent, lift. They were swept through the tunnel by the force of the water. Trying to cling to each other, they bounced off first one wall and then the other down the entire length of the corridor and came through dazed but unscathed. The force of the water diminished when it spat them into a larger cavern.

"We're getting close," Petia shouted in Giles' ear. "This is the second cavern from the entrance."

It was a large cavern, and Giles expected the water level to be lower—perversely, it filled rapidly. They found themselves struggling in swirling water up to their chests.

"What's happening?" Petia shouted. The panic returned in her eyes. She hated water but had coped with it. The mental vision of herself drowning proved almost overpowering. No longer did simple discomfort and her catlike aversion to water dominate—Petia now feared death.

"Don't worry, Petia. I'll get you out. There's got to be another way out."

Another surge of water entered the cave and swept them away. Turbulent water kept them off their feet.

"Do you know how to swim?" Giles asked.

Petia sputtered and blew water out of her mouth. "Just barely," she whimpered. "Cat paddle and float."

Giles swam to her, trying to use his wounded arm as little as possible. The pain gnawed deeper into the bone, burning as if the flame arrow still stuck in his flesh. Pushing away his own discomfort, he tried to calm her.

"You know the directions, and I know how to get you out of here alive. Believe it!"

But Giles was not certain that either was true. He talked Petia into turning onto her back. As she floated, he encouraged her to breathe regularly and calm herself.

"Giles, help!" At first, Giles started angrily to tell Petia she was safe. Then he saw the startled expression on her face. The cry had taken her by surprise, too.

The call reverberated around the walls of the cave, camouflaged by the roaring water, seeming to come at Giles from every direction, then echoed back again. But the voice was unmistakable: Keja.

Giles treaded water, peering across the boiling surface to find their companion. He failed to locate him anywhere.

"Up! Look up." Petia thrashed around, pointing. He calmed her, then scanned the walls, turning his body in the water with small strokes of his right hand. Finally, he spotted Keja. The small thief crouched on a spur of limestone near the ceiling.

"Get down, damn your eyes, and help me get Petia

out of the caves!'' Giles' mood darkened, and he had little time for Keja's games. With every new buffeting from the incoming water, Giles weakened just a bit more.

Keja clung to the rock, almost in tears. "I can't. I can't swim."

"O sweet gods," Giles muttered. "One can barely swim, one can't swim at all, and me with a lame arm." He scissored to the cave wall and found a spot to grab onto a stalagtite. Anchoring himself, he called out to Petia, "Stay here. Keep calm and stay afloat. I've got to help Keja." He waited until she nodded before proceeding.

Giles tried to keep his injured arm immobile as he used his right arm to begin the swim across the inundated cavern—impossible. Every stroke brought another sharp pang to the wound. Sometimes the pain was so sharp that Giles floundered and found himself sucking in water. Each time he roused himself, spat water, and took another stroke.

Each minor recovery took that much more of a toll on his strength. He faded rapidly.

The surface was awash with sticks, rags, clothing, wooden furniture, and twice Giles bumped his head against heavy objects, further sapping his endurance.

Petia floated, consciously willing her panic to subside. The Trans found herself trapped between her fear and loathing of water and seeing her friend vanish beneath the churning, white-crested watery death. Afraid to breathe, she forced herself to inhale calmly and exhale evenly. Her fear began to lessen.

With tentative strokes, Petia turned herself around in spite of the turbulence. Craning her head, she tried to find Giles. Only one or two torches guttered near the ceiling, making it difficult to see.

She peered through the dusky light and found him, low in the water, making each one-armed stroke look like his ultimate effort. Glancing upward, she tried to make out

Keja perched somewhere in the top of the cave. She couldn't see him.

Halfway across the cavern, a wave of nausea swept over Giles. His body twisted with spasms. He vomited once, then fainted, his head dipping underwater. The wound from the sparare had taken its toll.

Petia turned full attention again to Giles and his slow progress through the treacherous maelstrom. She watched helplessly as the spasm seized him. Petia did not hear the wracking gasps nor see him vomit, but she was aware of the sudden cessation of his struggles.

Face down in the water—he'd drown!

"Giles!" she shrieked. No response. He bobbed like a corpse. Petia gave a small moan that echoed back, mocking her. Forgetting her fear of the water, the cat Trans rolled over and began stroking clumsily but fervently. Her hands came down in front of her automatically, and paddled toward the inert figure, barely keeping her mouth above water. Her breathing gusted in quick and erratic spurts, but need drove her. Giles would die unless she reached him.

She thought that she'd never reach the floating figure. Determinedly, she kept on. Giles' body slammed against hers, driven by unseen currents, and Petia nearly succumbed. Fear came to her aid now, flooding her body with adrenaline.

"Giles!" she called. No response. "Don't be dead! Don't you dare!" She reached up with one hand and grasped his hair, pulling his head out of the water. His eyes were closed and blood trickled from his nose. Keeping his head elevated, she nudged his body with her chest. One hand in constant motion, Petia pushed him toward the edge of the cave. Luck favored her. A careless wave tossed them both high. Giles slumped over a rock ledge, arms outstretched. Petia clung to his legs until her strength returned enough to pull herself up alongside him.

"Giles," she yelled in his ear. "Giles, wake up. I can't swim out with you. You've got to help yourself." Tears mingled with the fine spray constantly drenching them. Petia shook him as she cried and swore.

From somewhere in the distance, Giles heard Petia calling his name. Why was she cursing him? So tired. Never before had he felt this exhausted. Why wouldn't they let him be? So damned tired.

"Go 'way," he muttered. Water rose in his throat, choking him. He vomited, losing both the meal and the filthy water he had swallowed. Panting, fighting to breathe, he slowly realized where he was, what had happened.

"Giles, wake up. Don't fall off the ledge. Hang on, Dismatis take you!"

"I'll hold you up. Won't drown. But so tired. . . ." Petia let go of Giles' thinning hair, and his head fell forward into the water once again.

The water seemed fresh and cool this time. But not in his nose. He lifted his head and snorted like a cetacean clearing its blow hole. His gray eyes opened and eventually focused. He shook his head to clear the hair from obscuring his vision.

"Giles, we've got to get out of here. The water's still rising!"

Giles looked at Petia as if she were some apparition come to haunt his dreams—his nightmares.

"Come on. Snap to, soldier." She slapped him as hard as she could. A kitten's paw held more force than her hand. "Come to. We've got to get out of here!"

"We've still got to rescue Keja." Old habits reasserted themselves. Soldiers did not abandon comrades. Petia's invocation of "soldier" gave him the needed impetus to carry on. He didn't have to think; he had experience to draw on. He pointed at the water washing over the ledge. "Find something floating. Maybe we could get him out on it."

Petia precariously stood on the slippery ledge and scanned the surface of the water. "There's a table. Would that work?"

"Perfect," Giles said. "I'll get it."

"You stay here and rest," Petia said. She slid into the water, more confident now, and paddled away toward the wood. She got behind it, grabbed the edge of the table, and kicked her way back to the ledge using the table for buoyancy.

"Sure you feel ready to tackle this, Giles? I don't need you fainting on me again."

"We don't have any choice. The water's going to fill this cave in damned few minutes, and we'll all drown. Let's get Keja and get out of here."

Giles scooted forward and lowered himself over the ledge. He floated for a moment, testing himself. Then, taking his place alongside Petia, he began to kick. The flow of water made it difficult to keep the table headed in the correct direction.

Keja crouched just above the water level, a stricken look on his face. "We'll never find the entrance."

"Calm down," Petia said. "Trust my sense of direction."

"Keja," Giles warned, "if you struggle, we'll have to leave you."

Keja's face went white as Giles explained how they intended to get out of the flooded cave. "Isn't there any other way?" he pleaded.

"None that I know of," Giles replied. "Now get on this table."

Keja slipped into the water and immediately sank beneath the water.

Giles anticipated it and grabbed his arm. Keja came up sputtering, beginning to fight blindly. Giles cuffed him enough to get his attention.

"Hook your elbow over the edge of the table, then stop struggling or I'll knock you inside out!"

The warning had its effect on the frightened thief. Keja had to try twice, but finally he lay prone on the table. Giles smiled to himself when he saw Keja's white knuckles gripping the edges. Afraid, yes, but not out of control. Giles admired that. Everyone who didn't have sand for brains was afraid at one time or another—true bravery lay in overcoming that fear rather than succumbing to it.

Keja and Petia both displayed real valor.

Giles looked at Petia to see if she was ready. She nodded, still frightened, and they began to kick, guiding the table before them. The churning water formed a vortex that tried to pull them off their support and down to the cave floor a dozen feet under the surface. Giles hung on grimly, dizziness hitting him again as the wound in his arm sent wave after wave of pain hammering into his brain.

"You're the guide, Petia. Wherever you say. I can't tell where the entrance is now. Cave's filling up. Water's coming in faster than I dreamed."

Petia cocked her head in what she hoped was the right direction, then started kicking.

It took several minutes to cross the cave, pushing the table before them. Keja wasn't a heavy man, but battling the turbulent water made the short swim frighteningly dangerous. Several times the table bumped into other large floating objects. Only constant encouragement from Giles convinced Keja to let go with one hand and guide the pieces out of the way.

When they smashed hard against the far wall, Giles shouted over the roaring water, "The entrance? Where?"

"Directly below us," Petia said in a choked voice. Her eyes widened as she realized what had to be done next. From the expression on Keja's face, he didn't understand.

"You can make it," Giles said. "Only a little bit more."

He turned his attention to Keja. "I can get you out of

here, but not unless you cooperate. Understand? We don't have time for arguing.'' The pain in Giles' shoulder sapped him of strength, but he had to go on. He reached inside and found reserves he'd thought were lost with his youth.

"Maybe we should wait until you've rested," Petia said, concerned at his pinched expression.

"No! Water's still rising. The sooner we do it, the sooner we'll be out. Then I can collapse." Giles tried for a lighter tone to reassure them. He failed.

"What do I do?" asked Petia.

"Hang onto my tunic, and I'll do the rest. Do you think you can do that?"

"Try me."

"That's it. Keja, listen carefully. We've got to dive down and find the cave entrance. The water flowing out of the mouth should sweep us right along. You've got to remember two things. Keja, are you listening to me?''

Giles got no response. Keja lay inert on the floating table, fingers white with the strain of gripping the edges.

Giles reached up and grabbed Keja's foot. "Keja, listen to me. Turn your head around so I know you hear me.''

Keja's head came around slowly, as if he feared that any sudden movement would deposit him in the water.

"By the gods, I'll leave you here, if you don't cooperate.''

Keja's head nodded vigorously, and Giles relaxed a tiny bit.

"Two things. First, before we dive you have to fill your lungs with air, take a deep breath. Second, I'm going to have my arm around your neck and you can't struggle. If you struggle, I'll let you go and you're on your own. I'm not going to drown for you. The going's hard enough without that.''

Keja's eyes were round, but he nodded again.

"A deep breath for you, too, Petia, before we dive.''

Petia nodded.

"All right, Keja. Into the water. Come on, just slide off and I'll hold you up."

Giles maneuvered behind Keja and kept him from going completely under as he left the security of the table. Giles felt a piercing pain, and another wave of nausea. With his injured arm, he reached up and around Keja's neck and gripped the collar of the thief's once fancy jacket. He glanced at Petia. "Feel down until you've got the edge of my tunic," he told her.

Petia's head bobbed just above the surface of the water when she said, "I've got it."

"Everybody get ready." Giles pushed away from the table, caught in the turbulent water like a leaf in a millrace.

The water closed over their heads. He turned underwater, looking frantically for the cave entrance. Some light would be showing, he knew. So far, neither of his companions had made a move. That was just what Giles wanted. He would need every bit of his strength.

Giles strained to keep his eyes open and find the cave mouth. As he searched, he weakened. Giles had overestimated his strength. The water tugged more insistently at him, preventing him from surfacing. More from weakness than design, he let it flow and tried to turn his body in the same direction. Lungs filled with liquid fire, at the bursting point, more pain than Giles could endure.

The water became a swirling current that turned the three of them completely around. It caught Petia's body and lifted it above Giles. Keja still hung in Giles' feeble grasp. All were tumbled about like stones in a lapidary's polishing drum.

Giles banged into the wall of the cave, and tried to kick against it to propel himself to the surface. The current caught them and carried them even farther down.

Giles had no more air in his lungs. Fat bubbles escaped

his nose and lips. Life faded from his body, even as he fought against it.

No! he mentally railed. Not only his own life depended on his abilities but those of Petia and Keja, also. Giles could die; he had lived a full life. But he could not take them with him. They'd trusted him, as so many soldiers had trusted him during the War.

He had failed many of them, but he had always given it every ounce of his soul, his very life in effort.

Once again Giles felt the flow of the water against his face. He edged into the main current, life departing his limbs faster and faster. Each movement became weaker than the one preceeding it.

Giles Grimsmate was dying.

Light shone wanly through the water. At first, Giles thought it was a death apparition, a visitation to prepare him for the gods.

More bubbles erupted from his lips as he tried to cry out in joy as he realized the cave entrance lay ahead!

He struck out with his good arm, fighting the current that swirled in crazy eddies away from the wall and tried to turn them back. Stroking desperately, he edged nearer the center of the flow. He felt less of the turbulence. He avoided the caressing hands inviting him to relax and give himself up to the currents.

No! Giles Grimsmate would not die this day! No!

The light became brighter, and Giles struggled to stay centered in the strong flow. He fought, but he had reached the limits of his endurance. With safety—and life!—scant yards in front of him, his tortured body rebelled.

Giles kicked feebly, then slumped in the water, the dim circle of light tormentingly close. The last thing he remembered before darkness constricted his senses was the burning inrush of water to his lungs.

Chapter Seventeen

The gods prepared him for death. Giles Grimsmate had eluded them for too many years. Now they claimed their due.

"Not so hard," he mumbled, then choked. Harsh hands plopped him onto his belly and slammed into his spine. He coughed up water and choked again.

This was what it was like meeting the gods in death?

"Giles," he heard a death messenger call. The gods wanted to be sure they had the right man.

"Here," he said weakly. "Hurry. I don't like it. Feels awful."

Another fit of choking seized him. Again the hard slaps to his back. Giles forced open his eyes, hardly daring to look into the face of death. All he saw was Petia on her knees behind him and holding him up.

"You, too?" he said, almost sorrowfully. Death claimed all eventually, but Giles had hoped Petia might escape.

"Welcome back," she said. "Are you going to be all right?"

"What?" Giles murmured. It took several seconds for him to realize his error. He still lived, and so did Petia. "Keja?" he asked. "What . . . ?"

"He'll be all right. Coughing his guts up right now. And probably praying to all the gods." Petia squeezed Giles' arm. "We made it. And mainly because of Keja. Without his aid, I'd've never gotten you out of the water. He saved both of us, Giles."

"Yes." Giles fainted again.

The next time he came to, Keja stood over him. The small thief's clothing hung in tatters and he looked drained, but otherwise seemed to be none the worse for the narrow escape. If anything, he seemed pleased with himself.

"We made it," Keja said proudly. "I actually swam ahead and pulled you and Petia free of the current."

"Not bad for someone who can't swim," Giles said, trying to sit up. Lightheadedness assailed him.

"Well," Keja said, eyes on the ground, "the currents favored me. They catapulted me past, and I just grabbed hold."

"Thank you," Giles said. The smaller man beamed.

"Do you think you can stand?" Keja knelt and put his arm around Giles' shoulder to aid him in what proved to be an insurmountable effort.

Both Keja and Petia had to support Giles underneath the arms to get him erect.

Water washed around their feet. The grass around them now lay flat and sodden. Giles saw the bodies of several drowned humans who had been swept out of the cave. He didn't want to think of how many might have been trapped in the cave.

Nearly carrying Giles, Petia and Keja made for a part of the forest where the ground rose. They found a dry spot and lowered Giles gently.

"Any sign of the sorceress?" Giles asked after he leaned back against a large tree bole.

"We didn't see her, but I wasn't looking either. Too many other things happening. Like staying alive." Petia knelt to check Giles when she saw his eyelids drop shut. He had slumped over and fallen into a deep sleep, so deep she couldn't rouse him.

Petia made a small fire while Keja retrieved their belongings from their original campsite some distance away. He strutted back, loudly proclaiming, "By the gods, I did it. By the gods! Saved you two, flooded the cave, and defeated the Flame Sorceress." Keja leaned back on his hands and sighed deeply, a sigh of self-satisfaction.

Petia aroused her own deep thoughts. "What? What did you say?"

"I was just congratulating myself on what a good job I did of saving you two and defeating the cult. I've performed some daring exploits in my life, but this is the greatest. The stuff of legends. Don't you agree?"

Petia turned her head. She stared at Keja, not completely certain that he was being serious. He appeared to be.

"All the work I did on diverting the stream into their air vents, entering the cave and getting you out of that flaming prison, then going back and getting an even bigger flow of water into the cave by digging open the vents—and killing another four or five guards. Finally, I returned to that dangerous den of devilment one more time." He smiled in contentment, the telling increasing his gloating. "The stuff of legends, or at least a folk tale."

"You're not joking, are you?" Petia asked in a quiet voice.

"No! Absolutely not. Danger everywhere. Daring rescue. I had to avoid hundreds of the human and Trans guards and also those flame things. I had to dig a ditch to get that water to the cave. All by myself." Keja should have recognized the quiet anger in Petia's question. He didn't.

"You take the credit for all that? Giles is lying near death with a wound in his shoulder, tossing between chills and fever, and you brag about what a wonderful job you did?"

Keja looked at her as if he didn't believe what he was hearing.

"Where would you be if Giles hadn't risked his life for

you? Perched up on some stone in the top of the cave? Oh, yes. You diverted the water into the cave, and it would have been your death, wouldn't it, if Giles hadn't saved your scrawny ass? You don't swim, remember? The gods ought to brand 'braggart' on your forehead, Keja. No air, the water rising, and poor little Keja crying out for help, and at the very last, with the water pouring into your mouth and nose, a whimpering child, a mere baby about to die." Petia stopped, out of breath from her tirade.

She put some more sticks into the fire. "You're not alone in this, Keja. Yes, you did a good job. But you didn't save us. Giles saved us. With a wound in his arm, he took two people with him rather than abandon either of us. One can't swim well and hates water. The other can't swim at all. Think about that for a while, Keja. Giles risked his life. If it hadn't worked, we'd all three be dead. Now just how wonderful are you?"

"I did get us out of the water," Keja said lamely.

Petia turned and walked off into the dark forest, disgust showing in her every movement.

Giles moaned in his comalike sleep. One arm thrashed out, and he threw his blankets away from his neck again.

Keja looked after Petia, torn between following her and staying to tend Giles. Keja was taken aback by her verbal attack. He had seen her angry only once before, the night he had caught her in his room at The Leather Cup. But that was different. Keja didn't really understand her attitude. He *had* saved them, when both she and Giles were too weak to do more than let the undertow pull them down to watery death. And he *had* diverted the stream, an engineering feat second to none.

Keja thought about what she had said, then shook it off. Women. Trans women. He snorted, leaned back and tried to sleep.

When Petia returned, she boiled some water and dumped leaves from the forest into it. She poured a mug and gave it to Keja. "Drink this. It's medicinal." Then she sat quietly by the fire without another word. Yawning, she rose, unrolled her blankets, and lay down to sleep.

Keja blinked in surprise at her actions. The tea tasted minty and soothed his throat. It seemed to help his stomach as well. Silently, he thanked Petia. She was a good woman, even if she didn't appreciate fully his finer points.

While Petia tended Giles' wound, Keja returned to the cave to seek out some sign of the key. Much of the clearing in front of the cave entrance lay covered with water several inches deep. The stream still poured out the cave mouth with the same force as when they had made their somewhat fortuitous escape.

Keja snorted in disgust as he sloshed around in the water. He saw no way to search the cave—not with the water gushing out with such a vengeance.

He wandered around the clearing, poking under the surface of the water with a long stick. Several human bodies had been washed out of the cave and lay with contorted limbs and bloated features turning them into something less than human.

"Poor disillusioned fools," Keja said. "Dupes. Deluded fools following a false dream, unlike the one I . . ." He cut off the beginning of another fine tale when he glimpsed a streamer of orange tangled around a tree trunk.

He waded across the clearing to find the body of a woman clothed in rich orange. Her auburn hair floated in disarray on the muddy water, straggling across her face. Keja reached down and brushed away the stringy hair.

"You must be the Flame Sorceress," he said to the corpse. Her lips were pulled back in the agony of her last minutes. She had drowned, just as many of her followers had drowned. She must have floated and been caught in the swirling currents within the cave. Finally, she had been thrown out of the entrance. But even battered, her beauty lingered.

"Thus ended her dreams of power, rebellion, conquest. Here in the forest clearing, water running around her. Twigs and bits of bark cling to her hair, washed down inside her gown. Food for water bugs. Like her flame beings, her fire has been extinguished." Keja allowed himself a thin smile.

"Not too bad. Think I'll tell some bard to include that in the telling of how I defeated the Flame Sorceress. Very poetic, very dramatic."

The Flame Sorceress lay on her side, one arm flung up. Keja turned her body onto its back. Open eyes stared up at him. He shuddered.

Avoiding her unseeing eyes, Keja searched her gown for pockets. He found none. He pulled the neck of her gown open, hoping to find a golden key on a chain or necklace. None.

He sighed. The chance had been a slim one. They now knew that the sorceress was dead and that the key was not on her body. He looked at her one last time. "A lesson in morality for the masses here," Keja said. "Greed and power seeking, vanity . . ." His voice trailed off. All that struck too close to his own motives.

"We've got to search the cave," Giles said. His fever had broken, and the wound was healing slowly. Petia's healing magicks with natural herbs had finally turned the tide against the Flame Sorceress' killing magicks infecting the shoulder wound.

"But the cave's full of water, flooded," Keja protested. "When I explored there earlier, the water still gushed out, no sign of stopping."

"How did it get that way, Keja?"

"Giles," Keja said in surprise. "The fever has burned overlong in your head. You know I stopped up the stream on the other side of . . .'' A sheepish grin came over Keja's face. "We need to divert the stream back. Or I will. You're not fit to do any work."

"We'll have to make it soon, too," Giles said. "The cult members from Dimly New and other temples will be coming on pilgrimages, to get their orders, for many other matters. Some guards outside the caves might have escaped. I don't want to explain to them how their sorceress died."

"I still think the key is in that throne room," Petia said. "It's just a hunch, but we saw several caves that seemed to be her home—unless she had sleeping quarters somewhere else."

"One step at a time," Giles said. "First, we'll get the water out of the cave. Then we'll have a little time to search. But not a lot. I keep thinking of all the cultists in Dimly New. The Flame Sorceress had them all primed for revolution. With her gone, they might take it out on us."

Keja had done a good job on the dam. Only a small trickle escaped downstream; nearly all the water had been diverted through the cave's smoke vents.

"I'll bet the farmers downstream are wondering what happened to their water supply," Giles said.

"They'll be up here investigating, too," Keja said. "I'd better get at it."

"Just roll a couple of those stones out of the way," Giles said. "The force of the water should help push the others."

The first stones came loose with difficulty. Keja struggled, pulling loose the branches and throwing them aside. Straddling the upstream row of rocks, he used his foot to shove more stones free. The water sucked greedily at the underpinning of the other rocks. Soon the force of the water assisted Keja in moving the rocks toward the original side of the stream bed.

"That's fine," Giles said. "There's so little that it won't matter. We'll just have to wait until the cave empties now. It will probably take a day or so."

The dank cave smelled like the insides of an oft-worn boot. Water seeped from cracks and crevices and ran in rivulets along the cave floor, and everywhere they found rotting debris. Petia wrinkled her nose disdainfully.

"It smells awful. I don't remember these odors before."

"All the water has released minerals from the stone. It will smell like this for months," Giles said. "The torch doesn't help, either." The guttering torch spat forth sparks as Giles held it high over his head. The strain tugged at his wound, but the others needed hands free for the search. His strength had still not fully returned and being the lowly torchbearer best fitted his abilities at the moment.

They sloshed through pools of water, stepped over bodies and saw dozens of burned spots on the walls—the only remnant of the flambeaux.

They pressed onward to the great hall. Giles' torch cast a wan light, which disappeared halfway down the hall. Along the walls the torches, now only soggy wicks, dripped waxy puddles on the floor. Black streaks, a mixture of ash and oil, ran down the walls.

An eerie feeling held the trio in thrall. Unconscious of their action, they pressed closer and proceeded down the hall, walking in almost reverent silence. The black onyx throne had floated free, only to be dumped unceremoniously upside down in the center of the room. The back had been broken. The beautiful flame carving was gouged and a large crack ran from top to bottom.

"Fitting," Giles remarked in a whisper.

They stepped around it and went on. The dais was covered with grime. A thin layer of slimy mud lay across the flooring, mixing with leaves and twigs left by the receding water. To one side they noticed a curtain, hanging limp and soggy. Petia looked behind it.

"Her sleeping quarters. A bed, nothing much else," she reported. "What sort of personal life did she lead?"

"She certainly missed a woman's greatest thrill—me," said Keja. Both Giles and Petia ignored him. They searched for another hour, growing increasingly dispirited.

"Is that the brazier you mentioned?" Keja pointed to the large brass urn, tipped on its side and barely visible beside a veritable mountain of mud, and separated from the carved wooden tripod that had held it. "The stand must have floated away somewhere."

Petia walked carefully across the platform, the footing slippery. She studied the overturned bowl. The curvature of the interior still trapped some water. She reached down and tipped the water out.

Frowning, she picked up the large bowl. The sound of metal on metal echoed through the stillness.

"What have you found?" asked Giles. He brought his torch closer.

"I don't know." Again, Petia rattled the bowl. It appeared empty but the metal on metal sound was distinctive. Holding it up, she saw fine lines at the bottom of the bowl. Cat claws slipped from protective sheathes and pried open the false bottom.

Laying in a tiny puddle of muddy water gleamed a golden key.

"The key!" she cried. It slid down the curve of the bowl and fell onto the dais. Petia stooped and picked it up. She held it up to the light. Giles and Keja silently looked at the object of their quest. All the death and destruction had netted them only this slender gold key. Giles let a moment's giddiness pass. The key hardly seemed worth the effort.

"Why didn't it melt?" Petia asked. "It was in the bottom of the brazier. The coals would have melted it!"

"Perhaps not," said Keja. "One lord I, uh, came into

contact with in a professional pursuit, hid valuables in a similar fashion. Did the brazier burn wood or oil?''

"I thought wood," said Petia.

"Oil," Giles insisted. "The colored flame came from different oils floating on the surface of coal oil."

"That's it, then," said Keja, crossing his arms and looking insufferably smug.

"What is?" Petia demanded, angry.

"The Flame Sorceress placed water in the bottom, then floated the lighter oil atop it. All combustion occurred in the air *above* the oil so that the key never got hot."

"Why put in water at all, if the flames stayed above the oil?"

Keja looked bemused. Giles cut in, "The bowl rim heated from the flames. The water insulated the key from the hot brass walls. What a perfect place to hide the key. Who would think to reach into a flaming bowl? What a devious woman she was!"

"Can we get out of here now?" Petia asked.

Giles laughed. It echoed hollowly around the haunted, darkened audience hall.

"Don't want to stay in this wondrous place?"

"Don't make fun of me, Giles," Petia said quietly. "We've found what we came for. Let's go."

Giles sighed deeply, and winced as the movement of his body tugged at his wound. "You're right, Petia. There's no reason to stay here."

No reason to stay amid the death and the suffering this religion had brought to Trois Havres, with ghosts flittering up and down the dank corridors. Like so much else in Giles' life, he sought life and found death. They had found the key. But the price. . . .

They left the hall and threaded their way out of the caves into the bright sunlight.

Chapter Eighteen

"There's nothing like a little sunshine to dry us out from our marvelous adventure, eh?" Keja almost skipped along the road leading from the forest back to Dimly New.

"You're acting like a little boy," Petia said.

"Why shouldn't I be happy?" Keja's grin and the slight duck of his head brought a smile to Petia's mouth. "Haven't we achieved all we'd set out to do? We've avoided the few survivors from the cave, haven't we? They are such a dispirited lot now. Don't care a fig for us. We have three of the five keys to the Gate, don't we? Let me revel in this! Rich! We're going to be rich!"

"You're forgetting, Keja," the Trans said, "that we lack two keys."

"Spoilsport," Keja grumbled, but his mood wasn't dimmed by Petia pointing out their need for two more keys.

"How are you doing, Giles?" she asked, looking over at the grizzled veteran.

"I'll make it." His shoulder was healing slowly, but it would be some time before it regained full power. The triangular scar that had formed would be a reminder, until he died, of the pain given by the Flame Sorceress' magical spear.

The trio emerged from the forest and slowly walked along the main road. The afternoon sunshine struck them directly, now that they no longer walked beneath the shade-giving trees. The distance back to the city melted away beneath their feet in spite of Giles' requiring several rest stops. He pushed harder than necessary, a vague sense of uneasiness nagging at him. It was too nebulous for him to trouble Keja and Petia, but it still drove him with almost desperate fury.

He wanted to be free of Trois Havres as quickly as possible.

As they came into Dimly New, Giles' disquiet turned to something akin to fear. In front of the Temple of Flame, a large crowd had gathered. Their mood was nasty, and Giles thought he knew why.

"Let's not look for trouble," Giles said. "We'll stay on the opposite side of the square and pass quietly."

"Do they know our part in their sorceress' death?" asked Keja. His earlier cheerfulness evaporated like mist in the sun.

"There's no need to stop and hear what they're saying," Giles said softly. "But it makes me think more than ever that we should just pack up and move on."

They edged toward the opposite side of the square. The man on the front steps of the temple was speaking loudly enough for a deaf man to hear.

"I was there," he shouted. "I saw it all. The stronghold of our Lady Sorceress is no more. It was flooded. Scores of humans and Trans drowned in the caves. The flambeaux expired—there are no more sacred flame beings! They were extinguished by the water!"

Someone in the crowd wailed, "The Flame in the temple has gone out."

"Our beloved sorceress," the man went on, "has not been seen in two days."

The crowd's murmurs denied any possible demise.

"She had taken two prisoners—they must have had something to do with the destruction I witnessed. I recognized one of the prisoners as a woodcutter we stopped a few days ago."

The man clenched his fists as he looked out over the crowd. His eyes flashed in anger. Suddenly he stopped his haranguing and stared across the square.

"That one! There he is now. The one who said he was a woodcutter and later was taken prisoner." He pointed his finger at Giles. "What do you say, unbeliever? What did you have to do with the flooding?"

"Nothing," Giles called back. "I escaped the flooding."

"How is it that you escaped and our people did not? What evil aided you? You're responsible for bringing an end to our hopes and dreams! What have you done with our beautiful Flame Sorceress? She would have led us out of our oppression. Answer that, unbeliever."

"She led you into a new oppression," Giles shouted back. "You were duped. Power was all she cared about. She held you in a grasp even firmer than you know."

"Liar! Desecrator of all that is holy! Destroyer of the Flame and the beautiful woman who showed us a way out of our miseries."

"Miseries be damned," Giles shouted. "Go back to work and fulfill your own promise. Work for your own betterment, don't depend on false promises. You were more slaves to her than you are to the city."

Petia plucked at Giles' sleeve. "Giles, please. Don't get egotistical like Keja. You can't win a crowd over, not with a trained rabble-rouser like that whipping them into a frenzy. It's going to turn ugly, and I'd prefer being elsewhere."

Petia was right. The crowd turned and began to edge across the square. Some stopped to pick up loose bits of brick and cobble.

"Come on, Giles," Keja yelled, tugging at the older man's arm.

Keja pulled him off balance as the first bricks began to fall around them. One stone barely missed Giles' head.

"Split up," Giles ordered. "You two run for the older part of town. Find an old warehouse to hide in. Petia, take our belongings. I'll meet you with horses outside the walls after dark. On the side that leads to Sanustell.''

"Will you be all right?" the Trans asked.

"Yes! Now run!"

Giles saw Petia take off at a dead run in the opposite direction. He started to dodge, but his weakness betrayed him. He stumbled and fell. To his surprise, a strong arm circled his waist and pulled him upright.

"Keja, I told you to go with Petia!"

"She's too much the cat for me to match. You're more my speed." Keja's aid helped Giles until he got his balance back and stumbled along, the screaming crowd at their heels.

"This way," Keja said. He turned the corner and ran toward the old part of town.

"Know where you're going?" Giles grunted with exertion. The sparare wound throbbed as if it were freshly inflicted.

"I know this part of the city from my tour of the taverns while you were up in the forest." He ran even faster, forcing Giles to a pace he could barely maintain.

The mob howled behind them. Keja ducked down an alleyway, then turned right when they came out of the other end.

Giles tried to keep up with Keja. His shoulder hurt more and more; his breathing was labored. "Gotta hide soon," he gasped out. "Shoulder hurts."

"Just a little more," Keja said. "You can make it."

Giles almost laughed as they stumbled on. Their roles had reversed now, from the flight from the water-filled caverns. After another five minutes of running, they no longer heard the crowd following them.

"In here." Keja stood at an open doorway, motioning for Giles to hurry.

Giles tried to speed up, but his body didn't want to cooperate. He staggered the last few steps.

Keja grabbed him and helped him across the sill of the

door. He turned and closed the door just as Giles slumped to the floor. Giles lifted himself up and looked around the interior of the room. Dust everywhere. Bales wrapped in burlap along one wall, untouched for years. Cobwebs in the corners and from the rafters.

"How did you find this place?" Giles whispered.

Keja held a finger to his lips as he put his ear to the door, listening. He motioned to Giles that they were leaving.

Keja shook his head and grimaced. "You think I was only drinking in taverns when you were gone up in the forest? There was this lass, you see, and—"

"Never mind," Giles said tiredly. Then, "I don't see any marks in the dust."

"You think you can make it up those stairs? There's a loft above and a place where I can keep watch." Keja reached down for Giles' arm.

Together, they climbed the stairs. In one corner lay a mattress filled with straw. Above it a shelf held a hairbrush and small bowls of cosmetics.

"I think your lass has been here more than once."

"No doubt," Keja said tartly.

He went to the far end of the loft and carefully peered out the dusty window. "No sign of any of them. I don't think the crowd can find us in here."

During the afternoon Giles slept. The wound bothered him more than he liked to admit, but it wasn't his first injury and it might not be his last. As all the others had, it would heal, leaving behind the triangular scar and a twinge when rainy weather threatened.

When Giles awoke, the men told each other stories of their lives to pass the time. Giles was fascinated with incidents from Keja's life of roguery and theft. Keja was equally taken with stories of battles and raids during the Trans War.

When the moonlight slanted silver beams across the loft, Giles said, "Time to be on our way. I had hoped it might be cloudy tonight. It looks too bright out for my taste."

"We'll be careful," Keja replied. "I can take us where we shouldn't see many people." He went to the front window to take one last look at the street. "There's city guard roaming around down there. Should we wait them out?"

"I think we ought to be moving," Giles said. "I'd intended to get the horses by now. And I'm getting a little anxious about Petia."

"You said yourself that she could take care of herself."

"Yes, I know. Still."

"We can go down into the alley by rope," said Keja. "What about your shoulder?"

"Let's look."

The pulleys and rope swung in place, a gentle night breeze teasing them.

"Can you lower me first?" Giles asked.

Keja grabbed the rope and snubbed it around his wrist. Giles grasped the rope with his right hand, then wrapped his ankle around the rope. Keja lowered him gently to the ground.

Giles ran the rope around his back and leaned into it, again using his right hand to grasp it. Keja descended a bit more quickly, but landed safely. He took the lead, and they left the alley.

"If we go by way of the waterfront, we'll probably have an easier time of it," Keja said.

For the most part, they were disturbed only by barking dogs along the route. The moon lit their way. In one section of narrow streets, where the moonlight failed to find its way, they crept from window to window. The lamps inside cast a dim light, but it was enough to see by.

They passed through the harbor area without incident. Giles wished that they would have simply taken ship from here; there was no chance of that now since Petia waited for them outside the city walls.

Keja began to curve inland again. Giles worried about how he would be able to get over the wall. They had agreed not to try the city gates, which closed at nightfall. Guards asked too many questions, and the last thing they needed was to be confronted by one who had become a convert to the Flame.

Keja began unwrapping a rope from around his waist.

"Where did you get that?" Giles asked.

"In the market, while you were asleep." Keja reached into his pouch and pulled out an iron hook sporting three nasty prongs. As they walked along, Keja bent to the task of fastening hook to rope. When he had finished, he showed it to Giles. "Thieves' knot," he said proudly. "Very handy."

Keja turned toward the wall. They came out of a dark street running perpendicular to the cracking stone wall. In front of them, Giles saw a long row of hutlike sheds with fronts that seemed to have no doors.

"The Market of the Poor," Keja whispered. "Dealers in junk, castoff clothes, vegetables and fruit that have been thrown away in the big market. I knew you would have trouble getting over the wall. But if we can use the roof of one of those hovels, and it doesn't cave in, you'll be halfway to the top."

They crossed the open street, and Keja pulled himself up onto the shed roof. He tested its strength, then reached down to assist Giles up. He coiled his rope carefully, stepped back a foot and twirled the hook around his head. A slight clink echoed through the night as the grappling hook sailed over the top of the wall.

Keja pulled cautiously until the hook caught on the outer edge. Using his weight, he tested it to make sure that it was securely anchored against the stone.

Giles watched in dismay as Keja leaned back into the rope and walked up the wall, more like a fly than a human. Giles peered up and down the dim street. If anyone were watching, he couldn't see them.

The rope dangled loosely. Giles looked to the top of the wall. Keja straddled it and waved down.

"Build a foot loop," Keja called down. "I'll haul you up."

"You can't. I'm too heavy."

"Don't argue. Just do it."

Giles fashioned a loop of rope, using knots he had learned soldiering. Even that small effort hurt his aching shoulder. He planted one foot carefully into it, then signaled Keja.

The loop tightened over his ankle as Keja began to pull. Giles hoped the rogue knew what he was doing. Unless he knew some trick, he'd never be able to lift Giles.

Giles grunted in surprise when he realized that he was no longer on the roof. He had been tugged a few inches into the air. He put out a hand and steadied himself against the wall. Again an upward tug, another foot gained. Slowly, a few inches at a time, he was being pulled up the wall. He glanced to the street again. At one end, he saw a guard with a lantern turn the corner.

"Keja. A lantern."

"I see. Just remain motionless against the wall."

Giles felt as if he dangled over the edge of the world, certain that he'd be seen. The lantern moved closer. Giles saw the guard more clearly, holding it before him and poking between the huts. Giles held his breath as the sentry passed by without raising his head.

For fully five minutes, Giles hung there. The light from the lantern eventually disappeared. Keja made no move to continue pulling Giles up.

"Are you there, Keja?"

"Just being careful. Ready to get over the top?"

Again the lifting started. Giles tried to estimate how

many more feet it was to the top. Giles was surprised. He realized that he was at the top of the wall.

Once Giles had a purchase on the top of the wall, Keja reached over and grabbed his belt. He hauled on it, and Giles found himself lying on top, gasping for breath.

"No time for that," Keja told him. "We've got to hurry now. The guard's going to change soon."

Getting down the other side was easy. Keja lowered Giles down, using his back and shoulders to take the weight. When Giles reached the bottom, Keja set the hook, and walked backward down the wall, using the rope expertly. With a whip of the rope, he loosened the hook and ducked out of the way as it came flying down.

"I think I'll keep one of these with me from now on," Keja said, wrapping the rope around his waist. "I wonder where Petia is."

"You don't suppose she left without us?" Giles said.

"I wouldn't think so. She's only got one key."

"She might not think it's worth the effort, after all we've been through getting this one."

"Don't think so, Giles. You're the one who said there was more to her than met the eye. Unless I misread her, that little cat enjoyed this more than either of us."

"You're right. There she is now." Giles pointed down the road running just outside the wall. "And she's got horses!"

Petia rode a horse and led two more, their packs neatly tied behind the saddles. She waved to them.

"What took you so long?" she asked, smiling wickedly. The moonlight caught her teeth and turned them into fangs. "I've waited for over two hours."

"Wanted one last look at the city," said Keja. "So many lovely wenches." The small thief's eyes sparkled as he added, "Are you sure this is your home? You hardly seem to fit in with them."

"Ride," Giles commanded. "Ride, both of you!"

Laughing, the trio rode through the moonlight, each with a key to the Gate of Paradise.

Keja broke into a bawdy song in a voice that made the others wince.

> *"Then the mistress of the house*
> *Said, 'My husband is a louse.*
> *Since the day that we were wed*
> *He's not taken me to bed.*
>
> *" 'Won't you come along with me?*
> *I've some things for you to see.'*
> *Then she took me by the hand,*
> *Took me to the starry land."*

In an inn along the city wall, a portly man rose from a table in his soaring tower room. His dark clothes went well with his swarthy visage. He peered down at the letter he had been composing, dropped his quill, and moved restlessly to the window.

The full moon illuminated the entire countryside beyond the city walls. He saw the Ahrome River valley sweeping down to the coast. A road crossed it and continued into the mountains; another road followed the river to join the coast road to Sanustell.

The dark man squinted when he made out three riders topping a rise in the road. For a moment, he watched them without recognition. Then realization of the identities of those distant figures came to him. The dark man called for a servant and gave him rapid instructions.

In a few minutes, he threw his pack across the cantle of his saddle and stepped up into the stirrups. His servant was still struggling with his own horse's bridle as the dark man rode off.

The dark man paused at the crest of the hill. Keja Tchurak's cracked voice raised in song carried back to

him through the still night. The dark man pursed his lips,
then emitted a shrill whistle.

From aloft came an answering cry. He held out a
gloved‧ left hand and whistled a second time. A black
form plummeted downward, landing heavily on the
glove. The dark man gentled the hawk as it tensed and
relaxed its talons on his leather-covered wrist.

"We'll keep our eyes on those three, won't we, my
beauty? They'll have little enough to sing about before
we're through. We'll see to that."

Keja's bawdy song faded as the three adventurers rode
on, but the dark man and his hawk followed them easily.

Soon. The dark man's time would come soon.

THE BEST IN FANTASY

PIERS ANTHONY